PREYING GAME

DECORAH SECURITY 2.0
BOOK 13

REBECCA YORK

OLIVERHEBERBOOKS

Preying Game Copyright 2017, 2025 © Ruth Glick

Cover design by Dar Albert, Wicked Smart Designs

Published by Oliver-Heber Books

This title was previously published

0 9 8 7 6 5 4 3 2 1

CHAPTER ONE

He was watching her, enjoying her pain. Alice couldn't see him, but she felt his appraising gaze as she ran on the treadmill, her sneaker-clad feet pounding the moving belt. The machine was not under her control. She could feel the belt speeding faster—faster. She gasped, struggling to keep up. If she fell, she would rub the skin of her leg raw.

Or she could jump off, but she knew the punishment for that. Dry cereal and water for dinner.

Gripping the handlebars, she forced herself to keep going. Her legs ached. Her heart pounded. She dragged in as much air as her lungs could hold. She wanted to close her eyes, but she knew that would be disorienting, and she might lose her balance.

Then, to her relief, she felt the machine slow. When it stopped, she flopped to the rubbery surface, feeling the ache in her leg muscles as she gulped in air. She lay for a few moments, using the hem of her tee shirt to wipe away sweat that trickled toward her eyes. When she felt able to stand, she tottered to the water cooler in the corner and filled one of the small, cone-shaped paper cups. Because it held very little, she had to repeat several times before she had quenched her thirst.

After throwing the cup in the trash slot, she heard the lock on the solid metal door click—her cue to step into the hall, where low-wattage bulbs burned in caged outlets. Once she had tried to reach through and unscrew a bulb. For her pains, she had gotten an electric shock. Now she kept her gaze fixed ahead until she came to her cell.

It wasn't like jail cells she'd seen in prison movies. Instead it was a bit more comfortable, with a single bed, a shag rug on the cold floor, a dresser with exercise clothing, and a shallow closet where nightgowns hung on wall hooks.

When she'd first come here, she'd been squeamish about getting undressed. She'd gotten over that when the dried sweat on her gym clothes started to stink. Still she never undressed in the bedroom—only the bathroom. In the small cubicle she stripped off her sopping tee shirt and shorts and dropped them in the chute at the side of the room.

She was sure he was watching her in here, too. Too bad about that. She had tried to find a way out of this nightmare. So far she had struck out at every turn. The doors were locked, there was nothing she could use as a weapon, and the block walls of her prison were solid.

When the temperature was adjusted in the shower, she stepped under the spray, enjoying the heated water pounding down on her body that was pale from weeks underground.

The shower was one of her few pleasures, and she made the most of it, shampooing her dark blond hair, then soaping her skin and rinsing until the water suddenly cut off.

With a sigh she stepped out of the shower and dried off, then toweled her hair as best she could and brushed it. She would have liked to cut it shorter, but of course he wasn't going to trust her with a pair of scissors.

She pulled on one of the nightgowns hanging in the closet and turned to the slot in the wall where her dinner was always delivered. Tonight it was bland chicken, mashed rutabaga, and green beans, without much seasoning—one of the standard meals. Healthy fare, she supposed.

The lights darkened to almost nothing as soon as she finished and returned the plate. In the dim light, she crossed to the bed, pulled the covers over herself and clenched her hands around the edge of the sheet.

Finally, she felt like she was alone, although she knew it was only an illusion. Closing her eyes, she returned once again to the fantasy that had kept her going.

Last year she'd read a book called **Wild Talent** about a boy named Paul Breen who could reach out with his mind and silently communicate with other people. In the book, the ability had caused Paul a lot of problems, and she'd felt sorry for the way his life had turned out. Now she spent every evening before she went to sleep trying to do what he'd done—connect with someone, anyone who could help.

Can anyone hear me? She silently pleaded. If you can hear me, please answer. My name is Alice Davenport, and I need your help. A man is holding me captive in some kind of underground bunker. I don't know exactly where I am now. But I was in western Maryland, working as a counselor at a girls' camp for the summer. I went off on a wilderness trek by myself, and he took me prisoner. He says nobody is looking for me, because they think I'm dead. But I'm not dead. This is me—Alice Davenport. He told me to call him Hayward. I don't know if that's his first or his last name, but I know he's going to kill me. I have to get away, and I need your help.

She repeated the message several times, praying that the desperate words could actually get through to someone. Yet, in the back of her mind, she couldn't help thinking she was a fool.

Like Alice in Wonderland, she had fallen down a rabbit hole. No one was coming to help her. She was going to be here until the man called Hayward chose to finish the game he was playing with her.

CHAPTER TWO

Jonah Ranger swiped a lock of dark hair out of his eyes and bent to inspect a ding in the teal blue paint of the 1955 Chevy he was restoring. Dad would have loved this car, he thought with a pang. But his father had been dead for ten years, leaving Jonah with a house that was too big for one guy and a collection of classic cars. Jonah had sold a couple of real beauties to finance his college education. After graduating and getting a job with the Baltimore city PD, he'd been on the detective fast track. But he'd hated some of the department policies. And he jumped at a job offer from Frank Decorah.

Decorah Security looked for agents with special talents, and Jonah had fit nicely into the program. There was an added bonus in working for the company. Frank had told him about a defunct auto repair shop in Beltsville, Maryland, near the agency offices, where he could store his cars and work on them. Plus selling the family home had provided more than enough money to buy it. He'd cleaned the trash out of the garage and the rooms above the shop, then turned the second floor into a cozy apartment.

Downstairs, he'd added the 1955 hardtop to his collection a

couple of days ago. Even the paint color was a special order on the vintage sedan that he'd bought from a collector in Georgia.

But the exact shade of blue was a lot less worrisome than the parts he needed for the 265-cubic-inch overhead valve V8 engine.

The radio was another problem. He'd thought it was working when he bought the car, but since bringing it home, he was getting a limited number of stations—with a lot of static. Every time he turned the dial, he thought he was tuning in what sounded like an old-time drama program.

Or was it? Through the static, he'd heard a woman pleading for help. He'd strained to make out what she was saying, but filtering her words from the background noises had been almost impossible.

Still, when she spoke, he felt a tingle along his nerve endings.

Tonight he was determined to pull in what she was saying.

He slipped into the driver's seat, closed the door, and grabbed the steering wheel with one hand, wishing the car had a modern headrest so he could lean back. Tension coursed through him as he fiddled with the station selector.

Once again, he was greeted with the familiar crackling sound—and then her voice. Only this time she was a lot clearer. Was it the atmospheric conditions—or what?

Can anyone hear me? If you can hear me, please answer. My name is Alice Davenport, and I need your help. A man is holding me captive in some kind of underground bunker. I don't know exactly where I am now.

Jonah sat bolt upright. "What?"

The woman who said her name was Alice continued to talk. Only now he knew that he wasn't just hearing the words over the radio. He was hearing them in his head. That was the talent Frank Decorah had seen in him and cultivated. Jonah could reach out and talk to someone—mind to mind. Not over long distances, but far enough so that he'd helped the Decorah team find kidnap victims.

But this was different. Somehow he didn't think that Alice was nearby.

I was in western Maryland, she was saying, *working as a counselor at a girls' camp for the summer. I went off on a wilderness trek by myself, and he took me captive. He says nobody is looking for me, because they think I'm dead. But I'm not dead. This is me—Alice Davenport. He told me to call him Hayward. I don't know if that's his first or his last name, but I know he's going to kill me.*

I have to get away, and I need your help.

"Alice?" He shouted her name into the empty interior of the car.

He was met with silence—and then her voice came to him again, sounding shocked.

You heard me?

This time, he didn't pick her up over the radio at all. The words were purely in his head—a mental transmission.

Yes.

Thank God. But how? I mean, am I just kidding myself? The first surge of elation evaporated from her voice, and she sounded like she hadn't really believed she could contact anyone.

His reassurance was instant. *I'm real. My name is Jonah Ranger. Where are you?*

I don't know.

In western Maryland?

I don't think so.

Why not?

I sort of woke up in the car while he was driving me here. I think it was a long ride. But I don't know in what direction.

He clamped down on his frustration and tried another line of questioning.

Okay. Tell me what you look like.

Why?

We're talking mind to mind—and it will help to picture you.

Oh Lord, like in a book I read. Only I thought nobody would hear me.

I did. But let's see if we can make the connection stronger. It's easier if I can picture you.

The voice turned eager. *Okay. I have dark blond hair. About shoulder length. My eyes are blue.*

How tall are you?

Five five.

He went back to her face. *What does your nose look like? Your mouth.*

My bottom lip is kind of full. I've heard people say my nose is thin.

Okay. And your skin?

Pale. I've been . . . inside for a long time. Her voice took on a warmer quality. *And what do you look like? I want to picture you, too.*

I'm six one. One hundred and eighty pounds. Dark hair—not too long. Blue eyes. Broken nose.

How did you do it?

I got jumped by some bigger guys when I was in high school.

I'm sorry.

It never happened again.

What do you do for a living?

I'm a private detective.

Just what I need. Or is this all too good to be true? she asked, her mental voice turning plaintive.

No. I can find you, he said, praying it was true. *But I'm going to need more information.*

Anything . . .

He thought for a moment. *He took you when?*

August

It was October now. Christ, that meant she'd been in captivity for a long time.

As though she were following his thoughts, she asked, *what month is it now?*

October

Oh my God. . .

From one moment to the next, the quality of the sound in his head changed. For a few minutes it had been loud and clear. Then it turned ragged.

Alice.

When she didn't answer, he called her name again and again. But he knew that the transmission had cut off.

Desperately he reached for the radio dial and twisted it, trying to get her back. He kept shouting at her, but now all he got was the freaking static.

CHAPTER THREE

Jonah? Jonah?

There was no answer.

As the sound in her head cut off, Alice held back a sob. Eyes closed, she balled her hands into fists, clenching them at her sides, struggling not to fall apart. For the first time in . . . months, she had felt hope. It had evaporated like drops of water falling on a hot griddle.

Tears gathered behind her eyes as she fought to bring her emotions under control. She'd been lying in this bed at night for an eternity, silently calling out for help. No one had ever responded until tonight. Then a man who said his name was Jonah Ranger had answered. That sounded like a real name. And it wasn't a name she would have made up—was it? She didn't know anyone named Jonah, or Ranger for that matter. But could she have read it in a book?

She squeezed her fists tighter, trying to work her way through what had happened. She'd called out to the universe, and one person had heard her. Unless she was imagining the whole thing because she wanted so desperately to grab onto hope.

She thought about the man at the other end of the connection. He'd said he was a detective, and he'd seemed like he wanted to help her. Then the contact had snapped. Could she find him again?

He'd said he was tall with dark hair and blue eyes. She liked that. And the picture made her feel closer to him.

He didn't answer when she called out to him now. But she had to believe that for a few minutes they'd made a connection.

Was it only for that brief time? Could she reach him again? When she tried, it felt like she was crying into a great void.

The frustration was like a horrible weight pressing down on her chest. It kept her awake for a long time, and she knew she was going to have a bad day tomorrow.

Jonah had slept badly, but he was anxious to speak to Frank. Some days the boss didn't come in, and Jonah was on edge until he saw the familiar gray Lexus pull into the parking area. Then he forced himself to wait in his own office for a few minutes before hurrying down the hall to the executive suite.

"Come in," Frank called out in answer to the knock on the door.

The Decorah head had to be in his late fifties, but he gave the impression of being at least a decade younger. It was like he'd discovered a secret way to tap into the fountain of youth—and that connection was keeping him in top shape. Now his keen eyes gave Jonah a speculative look as he walked into the small but nicely furnished room.

"Sit down and tell me what's bothering you," Frank said, reaching for the golden eagle coin on his desk. He leaned back, using his thumb to flip it in his hand.

Jonah sat, gripping the wooden arms of the guest chair until he ordered himself to relax.

"A woman called out to me," he said.

"You mean telepathically?"

Jonah nodded, thinking how casually Frank had asked the question. A couple of years ago Jonah couldn't have imagined having this chat with anyone. Then Frank had started a conversation with him in the bar at a law enforcement conference. Frank asked if Jonah often used intuition to solve cases. And Jonah was sure the man already knew the answer. They'd talked for several hours, off and on. When the Decorah head offered him a job, he'd switched from the public to the private sector in a hot minute. And he hadn't been disappointed. The other agents in the group had special talents that gave them an edge in investigative work. There were even a couple of other telepaths on the staff, Grant and Mack Bradley.

They and Frank had helped Jonah develop his skills. But he'd never had an experience like the one last night.

"Tell me what happened," Frank said.

Jonah told him about Alice's voice coming first over the radio, then directly into his mind. "The woman says she was kidnapped while working at a camp in Western Maryland. The man who took her made it look like she's dead. But she's really being held captive. She says she was taken in August."

"Lucky she's still alive."

"Yeah."

"And she doesn't know where she is?"

"Right."

"What's her name?"

"Alice Davenport."

"Maybe you should start with some conventional research. Is a woman named Alice Davenport missing? Is there a news story about her death?"

Jonah nodded.

"You also have to strengthen your connection with her and get clues to her location." Frank paused. "Perhaps you can even go there—in your mind."

Jonah blinked. "How would I do that?"

"Grant did it with Jenny Seaver when she was taken captive. As you know, he was eventually able to project himself into the room where she was being held."

"But he'd already established a relationship with her." In fact, the two of them were now married.

"Then your job will be harder. But you're not working blind. You know what Grant did is possible." Frank looked thoughtful. "I'll assign you to guard duty at the medical facility. Grant's working there, and you'll be able to get his advice."

Jonah nodded. "I guess I should do a little research before I talk to him."

"Yes"

Jonah left, glad that he had two attack approaches—talking to Grant and looking for evidence of Alice's abduction.

He left the office feeling more positive. As he combed through computer databases, it took a couple of hours for the hopeful feeling to evaporate. He could find no reports of a woman named Alice Davenport disappearing in Western Maryland—or anywhere else.

Well, actually, there was something he found in a decades-old newspaper article. But that was the only reference that came close. Plus he found no one named Alice Davenport who had recently been living in Maryland.

With a sigh, he pushed away from the computer and called Grant Bradley.

"Jonah," the other Decorah agent answered. "Frank said you might want to talk to me."

"Is this a good time?"

"Yes, I'm about to go to lunch. We could discuss the case while we eat. How about that Mexican place on Route 1?"

"Sure."

"Twenty minutes?"

"That works."

The two men arrived at the same time and asked for a quiet booth in the back. After ordering, Grant gave him a speculative look.

"What's up?"

"Frank didn't tell you anything about the situation?"

"No. I guess he wanted me to hear it all from you."

Jonah nodded, then filled Grant in on what had happened with Alice Davenport. He finished with, "But I can't find any record of a woman by that name disappearing."

Their food came, and both men turned to their meal.

Jonah swallowed a bite of fish taco before asking, "Do you think she contacted me to yank my chain?"

"Did she sound like she was in trouble?"

"Yes. But why doesn't anyone besides me know what happened to her?"

Grant used the side of his fork to cut off a piece of burrito. "Suppose she's like Jen? I mean afraid to give you her real name because that will lead to consequences she doesn't want."

"I guess that could be true," Jonah admitted.

"The abduction could even have happened in another state, and she pulled Western Maryland out of the air."

"Why?"

Grant shrugged. "I guess it would turn out to be complicated. Do you think she's had telepathic experiences before?"

"She sounded like she was doing it as a shot in the dark, and she couldn't believe she'd reached me."

Grant hit him with another leading question. "Do you think she was faking her abduction?"

He shook his head, struggling with new doubts. "It's hard to know. I mean, I don't have any experience with someone in trouble coming to me—rather than my getting the case as an assignment. That means I'm the one reaching out to the victims. And we don't always make contact. Sometimes I just had a clue about where they were—like maybe from seeing their surroundings."

"Yeah."

The two men finished their meals. Jonah signaled for the check.

"Frank said he was assigning you to the medical facility," Grant said.

"Right."

"So we'll be able to talk more. And you can ask me questions if you need to."

Jonah nodded.

"What's your next step?"

"I guess I'll try to make contact over the radio again."

"You think it will work during the day?"

Jonah shrugged. "I'm supposed to be working with you during the day."

"Frank already told me you might not be there until tomorrow."

"That won't leave you shorthanded?"

"We'll keep up the current schedule."

"Okay, thanks."

CHAPTER FOUR

Time for some fun, Arthur Hayward thought, as he leaned back in the comfortable chair in his book-lined library. Things had been going very well, but they had fallen into too much of a pattern.

He thought about his current guest in the underground portion of his estate. She was the best he'd ever worked with. Fit and able to improve. But soon she must reach even her limit.

He got out the pictures he'd taken of her when she'd first arrived. She had been in good shape then. Now she was beyond even his expectations.

She'd been groggy when he'd driven onto the estate and pulled into the three-car garage. He'd put her back to sleep with another dose of happy juice and taken her down to the examination room in the private jail he'd constructed.

First he'd taken off her clothes. Then he'd snapped some photos. He'd touched her body, stroking his hand over the silky skin of her thigh, the curve of her breasts, hoping the touch would stir him. He felt some kind of sensual awareness, but nothing like what he had felt in the old days.

As he pulled a modest nightgown over her head and slipped

her arms through the sleeves, his mind flashed back to his marriage. He grimaced, preferring to think of the present and not the past.

He knew Renee hadn't liked his hunting trips to game ranches in the West and safaris to Africa, but he'd set her up like a queen in this mansion.

When he'd found out the ungrateful bitch was stepping out on him, he'd started planning his first murder.

He'd done a superb job of pretending that everything was okay and that he wanted to share his African adventures with her. It had been easy to make her death look like a bad-luck lion attack—especially in a country where the rich white American was king. That was fifteen years ago, when the thrill of murder had not been his only sexual outlet.

For a ten years, he'd sampled the charms of many women, until high blood pressure had deprived him of the ability to function.

He gritted his teeth, trying to cut off the next thought, but it leaped into his head like a cat pouncing on a mouse. He had been about to say—"like a normal man."

But if you looked at it in the right way, he had never been a normal man. He had always been a cut above the guys who were content to live by the rules.

Too bad his moron of a doctor hadn't been able to do a thing about his blood pressure, besides putting him on pills that kept his dick limp, along with a goddamn boring "healthy diet." A diet he was sharing with his current guest, the lovely Alice Davenport.

He'd been able to observe her for weeks before he'd scooped her up. And he'd chosen her for her looks as much as her athletic ability. Why not destroy beauty as part of your pleasure?

All his life, he'd taken what he wanted. If he could no longer do it sexually, there were other ways he could attain the feeling of satisfaction. Once he had loved fucking women. Now he loved seeing them dead at his feet—after a long foreplay, longer than anyone could enjoy in a sexual encounter.

And soon the *pas de deux* would begin.

~

Alice had made contact with the man named Jonah at night. Was there any use trying to reach out to him during the day?

Maybe it could have worked, if she'd been able to concentrate. Unfortunately, most of her waking hours were taken up with tasks that required her attention. It might seem strange to think that physical training needed so much focus. But she had to stay sharp not to screw up. The facility where she was being held was large. Part of the complex housed a big gym. Weirdly, one of her jobs was bouncing a basketball on the wooden floor, then running toward the hoop and making a shot. Although she tried her best, she had never been good at basketball. And she was relieved when a whistle blew and she was allowed to return the ball to the rack at the side of the room and rest for twenty minutes.

Her next activity was different but no less taxing. A stout rope with knots dangled at one side of the gym, and she had to climb to the top and then down again. This time she had some leeway. She climbed more slowly than was strictly necessary, stretching out the task. But by the time she was finished with that, her arms and legs ached.

"Lunchtime," Hayward's voice rang out.

She sighed with relief, leaning against the wall.

"Shower first."

When he said the words, a shiver went through her. He only asked her to shower during the day when he wanted to meet with her in person. Was he going to declare that her training had come to an end? And then he would hunt and kill her—like he bragged he'd done with five other women.

She looked wildly around, wishing there was something she could use as a weapon. But she knew she was hardly going to assault him with a basketball.

On stiff legs, she headed for the corridor that led to her cell. There was no point in resisting. He would just hurt her if she refused to do his bidding. It flashed through her head that if he hurt her badly, maybe she wouldn't have to star in his diabolical hunt. But then what? He would probably be angry that he'd put in all this time training her—and gotten nothing out of it. She shuddered. What if he thought of some substitute amusement? Like killing her slowly?

Feeling as though she was caught between driving her car over a cliff and driving it into a bridge abutment, she stopped at the water cooler and drank several paper cups full. She'd been hungry when she'd finished the exercise session, but her appetite had disappeared.

Teeth clenched, she headed for her cell. As soon as she stepped through the door, her gaze swung to the bed. Confirming her suspicion, she saw that while she'd been in the gym, Hayward had laid out clothes. She saw a modest yellow blouse. A flowered skirt. Slip-on shoes. Surely he couldn't be intending to hunt her wearing those. Bringing the outfit into the bathroom, she got undressed, discarded her gym clothes, and stepped into the shower.

She clung to her analysis of the situation while she stood under the bracing spray. Again she dried her hair as best she could with the towel, then put on the outfit. The blouse and skirt fit perfectly. And she was sure they were a little smaller than the clothing she'd been wearing when he'd captured her. She'd lost weight on the diet he was providing and the exercise regime. The irony made her want to laugh. Like most women she knew, she was always trying to lose a few pounds. He'd forced her to do it—with no conscious plan on her part.

The door clicked open, and she walked back into the corridor.

"Take the route to the dining room," his voice boomed out over a speaker.

She closed her eyes for a moment, then made a turn to the right. Instead of heading for the gym or the exercise room, the route led her upstairs, and for the first time in weeks, she stepped into an area of the house that must be above ground. She glanced toward a window, but huge shutters covered the outside of the glass.

Another corridor beckoned, and she ended up in a room furnished with what looked like English antiques. She saw satin drapes, polished wood, velvet upholstery, and a table set for a meal. Well, two tables. Both were about the size of a card table, and they were separated by a metal grid that walled off her section of the room from the main part.

She looked around at the opulent surroundings and the food arranged on the tables. Did Hayward run this place himself? Were servants on duty, taking care of the dishes and the upkeep of the house?

If he had servants, what did they think about his holding a woman captive in the basement? Or did he pay them enough to keep his secret?

She looked toward the door at the far end of the room, feeling a mixture of fear and anger.

The door opened, and a man stepped through. Hayward, looking the way he had on the three previous occasions when they'd shared a meal. He was probably in his fifties, with salt and pepper hair, a pasty complexion, and dark eyebrows. His lips were a slash in the lower part of his face, and his chin was small for a man. He was wearing a tweed suit and a white dress shirt which was open at the collar. No tie. If she had passed him on the street, she would have thought he was pretty ordinary—and nonthreatening, but that was hardly what she would call him now. This man might look harmless, but she knew he was a monster whose greatest joy was wielding power over others.

She struggled not to let her emotions show or to glance away as she confronted him.

He tipped his head to the side as he studied her, a gleam of satisfaction in his eyes.

"You're looking fit," he said, a throwaway observation under the circumstances. She was in the best shape of her life because he had taken the choice away—for his own purposes.

"Have a seat, my dear."

The endearment made her want to snap out a biting retort, but she fought to control the impulse.

She sat down at her table, and he took a seat at the other one, facing her through the screen.

Plates were already set out, and she saw that lunch was steamed broccoli, chicken cut into pieces so she wouldn't have to use a knife, and half a baked potato with sour cream and chives. That was a special treat because she hadn't had a potato in . . . weeks?

Next to her plate was a glass with iced tea—another indulgence. There were even two sugar cubes in a little saucer beside the glass. She dropped them into the amber liquid and squeezed the wedge of lemon hooked over the top rim of the glass. Then she stirred, glad for something to focus on.

He had given himself the same food as she, although his skinless chicken wasn't already neatly cut.

He'd deprived her of a knife. But she did have the fork and the iced tea spoon. She eyed the cutlery. What if she took one of those and turned it into a weapon? Sharpen the handle of the spoon somehow?

The idea was tempting. She could slip the spoon or the fork into the folds of her skirt. But she understood on a gut-wrenching level that that would be taking too much of a chance. Surely he'd notice if either of the items was missing when she went back to her room. And then he'd be furious and retaliate.

So far he hadn't done anything to physically punish her besides making her work beyond endurance, but that didn't mean he wouldn't do it—or decide it was time for the hunt.

All that circled through her mind like a trapped animal turning in its cage. His voice brought her back to the present encounter.

"A nice healthy meal," he remarked with a touch of sarcasm in his voice as he cut off a piece of breast meat and forked it to his mouth.

What was this meeting all about, she wondered, as she took a bite of the chicken, forcing herself to chew and swallow? Was it tasteless, or had she just lost her ability to catch any flavor from the food?

Finally, he gave her a reason for their luncheon. "I'd love to get to know you better."

If she knew him better, could she use that to her advantage? "Yes," she managed to answer.

"I understand you were an English major," he said.

"How do you know?"

"I've enjoyed poking into your background."

The food in her mouth had turned to ground glass now.

Forcing herself to chew and swallow, she answered, "Well, I took as many American lit courses as English lit."

"Who was your favorite English author?"

What? They were going to discuss literature? She answered, "Thomas Hardy."

"Why?" he demanded.

"He was so good at rendering the lives of everyday people."

"How do you compare him to Dickens? Isn't he known for that?"

"Hardy didn't write as many books, of course. His subjects are always so dark."

"Dickens is dark."

"Not always. And often his books turned out okay for the characters you liked. He wrote **A Christmas Carol**. That's a classic feel-good story."

"True."

While they ate, they continued to discuss the books from her college courses. He seemed so well read, that she felt almost like she was having lunch with a professor. But she knew this was just part of the fun for him of holding her captive.

As the lunch progressed, he switched subjects and began filling her in on what he considered amusing historical episodes. One was called The Defenestration of Prague when a group of disgruntled assemblymen threw two imperial governors out a window where they fell thirty meters, landed on a pile of manure, and survived.

Hayward laughed. "A very colorful episode in European diplomacy."

Probably the imperial governors hadn't been amused, but she refrained from making any negative comments. As long as he was talking about long-ago events, he wasn't thinking about what he was going to do to her.

And even with all the undertones of danger, the conversation was a distraction from the barren life she was being forced to live. There were no books in her cell and certainly no television set.

The only bright spot had been the man who said his name was Jonah Ranger. And he might not even be real.

"What?" Hayward said sharply.

Her head jerked up. "What do you mean?"

"An expression I wasn't expecting crossed your face."

She felt suddenly cold. Until that moment, she hadn't realized how closely he was watching her.

"What kind of expression?"

"You looked . . . hopeful."

She managed to shrug.

But it seemed, he wasn't going to let it go. "What were you thinking about?"

She couldn't stop herself from saying, "I was thinking about how Hemingway felt emasculated by his wound in the Spanish Civil War, and how it came out in his writing, especially **The Sun Also Rises**."

"How did that pop into your mind?" he demanded.

She wasn't sure. But she was startled by the red flush that crept up Hayward's neck and into his face.

Scrambling for a reason, she managed to say, "I haven't focused on literature in a long time, but you gave me the opportunity to remember some of the classes I enjoyed. Like my Hemingway-Twain seminar."

"Are you sure you weren't thinking about someone coming to rescue you? Someone who could get the better of me."

Good God. How had he come up with that? "Who?"

"You tell me."

"No one even knows where I am," she said in a thin voice. "You made sure of that, didn't you?"

"Yes," he said drawing out the word. He was silent for several seconds, then added, "But maybe we should think about moving up our timetable." As he finished the sentence, he balled up his napkin, dropped it on the table, and stood.

"Perhaps you should get back to work."

She felt the food she had eaten congeal in her stomach.

"I enjoyed our talk."

"Did you?"

"Yes."

"I guess it did make a nice break in your routine."

His voice had returned to a neutral tone as he said, "Go back to your room, and get into your gym clothes. You can relax for a half hour while you digest your food. We wouldn't want to give you cramps. Then we'll have another session on the treadmill."

There was no use protesting that she'd probably throw up the meal she'd just eaten, even after a half hour of "relaxing." Instead she pushed back her chair, turned, and headed for the corridor that led to her cell.

CHAPTER FIVE

Grant had asked if Jonah could get in touch with Alice during the day. He'd only connected with her once, and that had been at night. But he supposed it was worth a try now.

Instead of heading for the Decorah office, he drove to the garage where he could reproduce the conditions under which he'd first contacted her.

After slipping into the driver's seat of the old Chevy, he turned on the radio. Leaning back, he reached for the tuning knob, then closed his eyes. He told himself it would be better if he relaxed, but his heart was thumping like a native drum, betraying his state of mind. As he turned the radio knob, he was greeted by static, the same as when last night's transmission had cut off.

"Alice?" he asked; "Are you there?" He spoke aloud and also projected the words in his mind, reaching out toward her, using the description she'd given him so that he could picture her. Dark blond hair. Blue eyes. A small nose. A sensual bottom lip. At least that was how he interpreted what she'd told him. She was five five. In his mind he made her slender and well proportioned.

He waited for endless minutes, keeping the image in his mind.

When he realized his free hand was clamped around the steering wheel, he made an effort to unlock it.

"Alice," he tried again.

She didn't answer, and he felt a terrible tightness inside his chest. Either she wasn't there or . . .

Or what?

They'd talked at night the last time. He imagined she'd been in her bed. Maybe there was something she had to do during the day. Maybe she was even with the guy, and she wouldn't be able to focus on a mental connection that had been heartbreakingly brief.

He gave it a couple more tries, but he suspected it wasn't going to do any good. He'd have to wait until she had some quiet time. Then she'd be able to reach out to him again. Or not.

A wave of cold swept over him. She'd done it once. There was no reason to think that she couldn't repeat it. Unless it had something to do with atmospheric conditions and radio waves.

After a few more minutes of trying to reach out, he gave it up. Disappointment was like a damp, heavy blanket weighing down his whole body. With a sigh he turned off the radio and levered himself out of the car. Unable to stop himself, he slammed the wide door in frustration. Maybe he should go over to the Decorah medical facility and make himself useful.

By the end of the day, Alice was staggering around like a drunken nightclub patrol. Hayward had worked her so hard that she could barely change into her nightgown and carry her dinner tray to the table in her cell. The meal looked particularly unappealing tonight, but sending the food back untouched was not an option. This was all she was going to get, and she knew she had to eat while she could. Doggedly, she forced herself to chew and swallow the vegetables and chicken that had the texture of rubber.

After she finished the meal, she put the tray in the slot and fell into bed.

She lay in the dark, somewhere between sleeping and waking. In her present state, it was almost impossible to believe that Jonah Ranger was real. It made sense that she'd conjured him up because she desperately needed some shred of hope in her awful existence.

But he had given her a connection outside her prison, and as she lay in her bed, she gathered her strength to reach out to him.

This time it was the other way around. She heard his voice ringing out in her head.

Alice?

In the dark, she blinked. Was that really him?

She wanted to call his name out loud. But that would be a mistake. Probably Hayward was listening to her, and he'd want to know who she was talking to.

Instead, she kept the answer in her mind. *Jonah?*

Yes

Thank God.

That's what I was going to say. I tried to reach you at lunchtime, but it was a total bust.

She thought back to her own lunch. *Hayward made me eat with him in the formal dining room. I had to focus on the conversation. We were talking about literature and history. Something I said made him angry, and he worked me so hard I almost fell over.*

Angry about what?

About you.

He felt a surge of alarm. *You didn't talk about me, did you?*

No. I wouldn't do that. She gave a mirthless laugh. *But I thought of you, and he said my expression had changed. He said I looked hopeful. And when I tried to pretend I was thinking about something else—that didn't work out so well either.*

Jonah answered with a curse on the other end of the line. *Sorry.*

That's okay. I agree completely.

What was the other thing you said?

Hemingway popped into my head. I, uh, said I was thinking about how he felt emasculated after the Spanish Civil War—and that came out in his writing.

Interesting. You think the guy's impotent? That could be a reason he gets his kicks from keeping you captive.

I don't know. But he did flush when I said it.

I'll file that away. But we'd better get back to work, in case we lose the connection again.

That made her heart pound. *Oh Lord, I hope not.*

I have to ask you something.

The urgency in his voice grated against her nerve endings as she tried not to focus on her fear. *Okay.*

Is Alice Davenport your real name?

Yes.

I can't find any record of your having gotten killed.

You can't?

Jonah hesitated for a moment, then asked, *Is there some reason you don't want me to know your real name?*

Of course not.

She sounded sincere. But he supposed she would if she had a reason to keep her identity secret. He wanted to press her on that, but he thought it would be a mistake. What if he scared her, and she cut off the communication? But why would she? She was the one who had begged for his help in the first place.

He put the puzzle of her name aside and focused on the

verbal picture she'd given him. On her dark blond hair, her blue eyes, her pale skin.

He'd been unconsciously leaning toward the radio. He forced himself to relax in the seat. Screw the identity part. The important thing was to get her out of there. Unless this was some kind of con. Too bad he couldn't record this conversation and let the other Decorah agents listen to it. But it was all in his head. There was nothing to record.

You say he's going to kill you.

Yes!

How do you know?

He told me.

He could be lying.

He told me he's killed five other women.

Jesus!

You said I've been here two months.

Yes. Has he hurt you, he asked, dreading the answer.

No. What he's doing is giving me physical training. Running. Climbing. Stuff like shooting baskets. Climbing a net. Once he thinks I'm ready, he's going to turn me loose outside—at least I think it's outside—and hunt me. We're in a big house. I'm assuming it's on a big estate. And I guess it's in an isolated location.

What? he gasped. Just to make sure he'd heard her right, he repeated what she'd said. *He's going to hunt you and kill you?*

Yes, she answered again.

That's ... inhuman.

Yes. Like I told you, nobody knows I'm here. He says they think I died in a freak rock slide and I'm under thousands of tons of rubble.

Christ!

I get meals in my cell. Someone cooks them, but maybe it's him. *They're awful. No salt. No seasoning. No frying. I suppose it's what you'd call healthy food.*

Is there anything you can tell me that would help me find you?

There was a long pause on the other end of the line, and his pulse pounded in his temple. Last time the conversation had cut off abruptly. Was she still there?

Alice?

I'm sorry. I can't think of anything. He sensed her dragging in a breath and letting it out. *Okay, well, it's an old house, I think. Or made to look old. In the dining room the furnishings are antique. Or they're good reproductions.*

What can you see out the window?

Nothing. The shutters are closed.

Damn. Do you know when he's planning the hunt?

No, but like I said, he implied he might move it up.

We'll figure out how to get you away from him. He wanted to believe it. He knew she did too.

Her mental voice turned tentative. *I asked you a little about it last night. How is it that I'm able to talk to you like this?*

He cleared his throat, then realized he was only stalling for time. *This may sound weird, but I work for a security agency where a lot of the agents have . . .* he tried to think of how to put it. *Special powers.*

You mean superpowers? Like Superman or something?

Now he heard the skepticism in her inner voice.

Not like superheroes, he answered quickly. *Frank Decorah, the man who runs the agency, recognizes people with unusual talents. There are several of us who can communicate mind to mind. I'm not the best at it. I've used the talent to help find kidnap victims. But in the past, it was always over short distances.* He sighed in frustration. *I don't even know where you are.*

Right. But how did we . . . make contact? I mean, I was sending out a message in my mind, hoping against hope that someone would hear me.

And I did. I was working on a car. I kept getting static on the radio. And then I heard your voice. I don't know how it happened, he added quickly. *But somehow it was the reverse of what I've done in the past. You reached out to me.*

Not to you, she put in quickly. *I was desperate for someone to help me. And you were there. Thank God,* she added.

Yes, thank God.

When he'd found kidnap victims before, he'd done it by lying down in a dark room with his eyes closed and sending his mind out to a victim that Decorah Security was trying to find. The link might not be strong. But he could strengthen it by getting physically closer, usually in a van—with someone else driving. He had always been the active agent in reaching out. And sometimes he'd established a rapport with the victim. But he'd never felt as personally connected as with Alice. He wanted to keep talking to her now. But when he looked at his watch, he was shocked at the time.

It's after 1:00am he said.

That's late. I have no way to tell time here.

If you're going to be doing physical stuff all day, you have to get some sleep.

I know, but I don't want to stop talking to you. You're the only human contact I've had since I got here . . . except with him. Please, can you stay a little longer?

Feeling her desperation, he could only say *yes.* And he didn't want to break the connection either.

Tell me about yourself, she said.

He thought about what to say. *You know I work for a security company. I have a degree in criminal justice from the University of Maryland.*

Why didn't you go into the police force?

I did. Then I met Frank Decorah, and his agency seemed like a better fit.

Tell me something fun about yourself.

The first thing that came into his head was, *I'm really good at Monopoly. We had a club at my school.*

Oh, me too. My brothers and sister and I loved to play. Do you have siblings?

No. I was an only child. My Mom was a teacher in Baltimore. My dad worked for the Social Security Administration. They're both gone.

I'm sorry.

Decorah Security is like my family now, he answered, thinking how lucky he was that Frank had sought him out. *Tell me about yourself.*

I'm pretty ordinary.

I don't think so. He must have picked you for a reason.

Maybe because I'm athletic. I grew up on a farm.

You did?

Uh huh. I had two brothers and a sister. My dad probably wished more of us were boys, but we all had to pitch in with the chores. I milked cows, fed chickens, collected eggs.

Sounds like fun.

Anything sounds like fun if you don't have to do it every day.

He was about to ask another question, when he heard her gasp.

What?

I think he knows I'm awake. Oh Lord, I have to go.

Before he could say more, she broke off the conversation, and he felt like one of his arteries had been severed.

CHAPTER SIX

"Alice," Jonah shouted. Something had happened. Something bad.

She'd said the guy knew she was awake. And what? He was angry? He was going to hurt her? He *was* hurting her now.

Jonah called her name into the darkness.

He had to get back there. Or was he wrong? Maybe, under the circumstances, trying to reconnect was worse than leaving her alone. And maybe he couldn't do it by himself anyway. Not if Alice was blocking him. Or unconscious or something else bad.

He didn't *know*.

But he couldn't do nothing.

Trying to calm the frantic pounding of his heart, he struggled to reach out to her again. Now it was like there was no substance to grab onto. She was gone.

For twenty panicked minutes, he kept trying to get to her again. By the time he knew it wasn't going to work, his body was dripping with sweat, and his blood pressure was probably in the stratosphere.

Heaving himself up, he pulled on running shoes and shorts,

pounded down the steps, and stepped into the chilly night air. He started running, as hard and as fast as he could, striving to empty his consciousness of everything but the pounding of his feet and the breath gasping in and out of his lungs. He had never pushed himself so hard. When he was reduced to staggering, he turned and made his slow way back to the old garage.

Inside, he dragged himself up the steps, took a hot shower, then flopped into bed where he slept like a drugged mental patient, too exhausted to let his mind keep churning.

He woke with a start a few hours later, remembering everything and ordering himself not to go crazy again. Turning his head, he looked out the window and saw the gray light that comes before the sun is up.

He'd tried to reach out to her in a panic and failed.

Was there any use trying again?

"Don't force the connection," he ordered himself. "Picture her instead."

This early, she would still be lying in bed—if the guy hadn't dragged her off somewhere.

Gritting his teeth to slash away that last thought, he went back to picturing Alice. He dressed her in a modest nightgown and imagined she was in a small, whitewashed room, her eyes closed, her blond hair tousled on the pillow.

Once he had gotten that far, he allowed himself to hope for more. If her mind was closed to him, what if he could make a different connection?

He knew that Grant had been able to join Jenny in her bedroom when she'd been abducted. Not with his body but in a sort of spectral form—the next step after contacting her telepathically. At first he'd had no real substance in the room where she was being held, a ghost only she could see. But he was able to make himself more solid, and finally it was like he was really there.

Of course, Grant had had a big advantage. He'd known Jenny a lot better than Jonah knew Alice. Probably he'd already made love with her, Jonah thought with a pang, which would give him a strong physical link. Plus, he knew her location because he'd had a tracker on her car and been able to drive within a few miles of the estate where she was being held. Outside the grounds, he met with Decorah agents who had rented a house where he could lie in bed and reach out to her.

That was before Jonah had joined Decorah Security. But Grant had told him about the experience when he'd helped Jonah learn to use his psychic talent.

Now the whole idea sounded impossible. He never would have considered it in a million years, unless he knew someone who'd already done it. Luckily he had Grant's success to use as a model.

Jonah might not have the advantages of knowing Alice's location or having been intimate with her. But he was as desperate to contact her as Grant had been with Jenny.

He gathered up a fist full of sheet and squeezed it in his hand.

Was he crazy enough to think he could do something so outside the realm of normal human experience?

Yes. Because his conversations with Alice fell into the same category. And what did he have to lose by trying?

He laughed and unclenched the sheet. If he really thought he could go where she was, maybe he should put on some clothes.

He got up and pulled on a pair of comfortably soft, faded jeans over his boxers and got back into bed. When he was ready, he took a deep breath and let it out, then squeezed his eyes shut, feeling his muscles tense.

"Stop it," he muttered to himself. "Tension isn't going to help. Loosen up."

He made a conscious effort to relax and went back to picturing Alice lying in her cell.

He could bring up the scene, but he couldn't get any farther. He was still lying in his own bed.

He swung his head toward the clock on the bedside table. 6:00 am. It was tempting to call Grant and ask for advice. But he was pretty sure his friend couldn't tell him how to do this. He'd have to figure it out for himself.

Suddenly he had an inspiration. He'd taken some courses in self-hypnosis. When he was in the hypnotic state, he'd travel to a private place where he could veg out.

Could he extend that trip to Alice's location?

Recalling the techniques he'd learned, he opened his eyes and looked up to the line where the ceiling and the wall met.

"Relax now . . . relax now . . . relax now," he told himself, feeling the phrase trigger the familiar weightless sensation of going into a trance. It came with a kind of buzzing in his brain that extended to his body.

It was as if his physical self was no longer as important as his mind. Which meant he could leave that part of himself lying in bed. Usually he went to a quiet beach where he could lie in the sun and listen to the sound of the waves breaking on the shore. He landed on the beach now and stayed there for a few minutes, lounging on a comfortable chaise, enjoying the breeze, the waves, and the feel of the warmth on his skin. It was so peaceful here that he felt sluggish. But he got up and slowly walked into a small beachcomber's shack that was several yards back from the water, surrounded by leafy vegetation.

Inside was a staircase. Of course it would have been impossible to really descend into the earth so close to the ocean. Water would have been lapping a few feet below the floor. But he was in a hypnotic trance, and the rules of the natural world had no power in this place.

Trying to keep hold of the peaceful feeling, he slowly descended the stairs, using the image of walking down to pull himself deeper into the trance—and to get him to Alice, since she'd said she was in an underground facility.

The bottom of the stairs was dark, but he saw a light shining from somewhere close. When he reached the lower level, he found he was in a corridor underground, like the corridor Alice had told him led to her cell. The light was muted, with bulbs in cages overhead. Was this really where he would find her? Or was he making all this up because he wanted to be here?

It hardly seemed possible that he had actually gotten to her location—after completely losing the connection with her a few hours earlier.

Still, he followed the corridor to the end, where he found a heavy metal door with a lock and a horizontal slit, like a pass-through for dangerous prisoners.

There was a small window in the door. When he looked through, he saw a woman lying on a bed, her eyes closed.

He had no substance in this place, and there was no way to open the door. But if he could do the same thing Grant had, he didn't need to open it. Putting up his hand, he pressed against the metal surface, watching with awe as his flesh went through the barrier. He closed his eyes and stepped forward. There was no feeling of resistance. But after several steps, when he opened his eyes, he was on the other side of the door.

Elation surged through him. Still he didn't trust the experience? Was he really where Alice was being held? Or was he making all this up because he wanted it so much?

As he stared at the woman on the bed, he saw her body jerk and her eyes fly open. They focused on him, and he heard her make an exclamation.

"Oh my God."

He knew from the look of shock that bloomed on her face

that she could see him standing in the room. Or, more accurately, she was seeing the image he had created in his trance. *Yes*.

For a few electrified seconds, they stared at each other, as though neither of them could believe what had happened.

Was there a way to find out if it was real?

When he took a step forward, the scene wavered.

Madly he shouted, "No."

But it was already too late. He was back in his own bed, lying on his back with his heart pounding and his breath coming in uneven gasps.

His curse rang through the room. All that effort—and it had come to nothing.

Once again, he calmed himself.

No, he corrected. It hadn't come to nothing. He'd been in her room—her cell. And Alice had known he was there.

She had looked as shocked as he had felt. But that proved nothing, he cautioned himself, not if he was making the whole thing up—like a beach where there was no water below the surface of the ground.

The only way to prove it was real was to go back there. He had done it once. He could do it again.

He closed his eyes, willing himself to be calm. But now his pulse was pounding in his temple, and he knew he had lost the slender connection again.

CHAPTER SEVEN

The door of Alice's cell slammed open, and Hayward stepped in, his eyes blazing. He was holding her breakfast tray, the tray he brought every morning. But he had never stepped into her cell before.

His gaze flew around the room. "Now what's going on?"

"Nothing."

"Is someone in here with you?"

She stared at him as though she thought he'd lost his mind. "Someone with me? How could there be?"

"You tell me?"

She could only shake her head. There was obviously nobody else in the room except her captor.

"What was that I heard?" he pressed.

She improvised quickly "Well maybe I cried out or something. I think I was having a nightmare. You woke me up." Struggling to keep her expression neutral, she didn't lower her gaze.

Hayward had never risked getting close to her without a barrier. She tensed, wondering if she had a chance to take him down. He'd been forcing her to get into the best physical shape she could imagine. She was stronger and faster than she ever had been in her life. Maybe that would make a difference.

Then he shifted the tray, and she saw the gun in his hand. If she lunged at him, she'd be dead before she could make it across the room.

Perhaps a week ago, she might have done it anyway. It would be over quickly—all the torture and the threat. Now she had a reason to hope she could get out of here alive.

"What does that look mean?" he asked.

"I don't know. Maybe the isolation has finally made me crack up. Or you could be driving me crazy with your infernal routine."

He seemed shocked. She'd tried to think of little ways to defy him, but she'd never challenged him before.

His gaze turned speculative. "You've changed. Why?"

She shrugged. "Why do you think so?"

He took a step back. "I'm not going to share my thoughts with you."

She knew he was shaken, but he kept the gun pointed at her as he set down the breakfast tray on the table, then backed out of the room and locked the door behind him.

She moved to the table and picked up the glass of orange juice on the tray, sipping as she thought about Hayward and this telling encounter. He had so enjoyed being in charge of this whole scenario. Yet it hadn't taken much to jack his confidence down a notch.

It made her think that, in reality, he was a coward who enjoyed exercising power over people who couldn't challenge him. Perhaps she'd stumbled on the truth when she'd come up with that emasculated stuff.

As she alternated juice with scrambled eggs and dry wheat toast, she switched the focus of her thoughts.

Hayward had come in with such a menacing posture that

he'd captured all her attention. He'd been her nemesis for weeks. Not only that, he'd been the center of her universe. But no longer. That role had switched to Jonah Ranger, the other man who had been here this morning.

She'd been asleep, dreaming of Jonah—of his lying beside her in bed, holding her and kissing her and telling her everything was going to be okay. Then she felt a change in the air in the room, opened her eyes, and saw someone standing by the door. *Him.*

He looked the way he'd described himself, with dark hair and blue eyes. Bare-chested, dressed in a pair of faded jeans.

He hadn't been exactly solid, she thought, as she brought the image back. Knowing it was Jonah was more than a question of his appearance, though. She sensed it because she felt a connection between the two of them that was almost supernatural.

She couldn't hold back a small laugh, and wondered if Hayward was listening for her to say something in here. What did supernatural mean exactly? She knew Jonah wasn't a ghost. But at the same time, it was impossible for him to be here in reality. The mental link between them had brought him. Well, not just that. She suspected he had put out some kind of superhuman effort to get to her cell. That knowledge was like the warmth of the sun finally shining into this underground room. He had cared enough to somehow reach her. And she prayed that he could do it again.

She wanted to lie back down on her bed and open her mind to him—inviting him to return. Surely that would make the process easier. But at that moment a bell rang, and she knew that her breakfast time was over. She had to get ready for the day. And she had to be alert for anything that could help Jonah get her out of here.

As she dressed, her thoughts switched back to Hayward.

He'd told her he'd gone to Africa and hunted big game. And he'd said that hadn't been enough of a challenge for him. He'd told her he wanted to hunt the ultimate prey. And without worrying about the morality of taking human life, he'd done it. In cold blood. With a lot of preparation.

He looked physically fit. But his mind was like a nest of snakes. And that made him dangerous in ways she couldn't even imagine.

Jonah lay on his bed, breathing hard. He had done it. Against all odds, using self-hypnosis, he had sent his apparition to Alice's prison. He'd materialized outside her room, stepped through the solid door, and managed to stay there for a few seconds, until the bastard who kept her captive had showed up. That had been enough to break the link with her.

But if he'd done it once, he could do it again. He settled the pillow comfortably under his head and went through all the steps he'd followed earlier. Putting himself in a trance, going to the relaxing beach, descending the stairs to the corridor that led to her cell. But this time the light in the hallway was dimmer. It was like he wasn't quite there. And when he walked to the door of her cell and pushed his hand against it, he met resistance. He shoved harder, changed the angle, pounded his fist, but none of it worked. This time there was no way to get through the door.

Exerting his will in this twilight place only gave him a headache.

"Shit," he muttered as the whole scene flickered out of existence.

Apparently he couldn't just come here on his own. Alice had to be ready to receive him. And probably now she was busy.

Working out, he thought with a snarl. The bastard was making her push herself to her physical limit.

Jonah sat up and ran a hand through his hair. After a lot of effort, he'd managed the initial trip to her cell on his own. But now she knew he had done it, and hopefully she'd be able to reach out to him—the way she had that first time on the car radio.

Realistically he knew he'd have to wait until she was alone and receptive. Which probably meant tonight.

He cursed again. How was he going to get through the next ten or twelve hours waiting to try it again?

He went for another long run along the country roads near his auto shop, this time at his normal pace. The activity made him feel closer to her. Maybe she was doing the same thing.

Back home, he stopped beside the Chevy and put his hand on the flat roof, thanking God he'd bought the car. If he hadn't done it, he was sure he wouldn't have hooked up with Alice.

Upstairs, he showered and dressed.

At a Starbucks in a shopping center on Route 1, he got a coffee and a breakfast sandwich. Bringing the food with him, he drove to the Decorah medical facility.

Grant was sitting at the security station when Jonah walked in. He looked up and gave him a considering look. "I'm guessing you've had some success with Alice."

"How do you know?"

"Your attitude. You seem . . . calmer. And more confident."

"Yes and no."

"Sit down and tell me about it."

Jonah took the other chair and put his food on the counter. He was taking a sip of coffee when Grant asked,

"You know where she is?"

"Not yet, but I took a page from your playbook."

"As in?"

"I went to where she is. The way you went to Jenny when she was being held captive. I never would have considered trying it—except that I knew it had worked for you."

Grant's eyes lit up. "Way to go. How did you do it?"

"Self-hypnosis."

"Clever. *I* wouldn't have thought of that."

"But you had the advantage of already being with Jenny," he answered, not making a big deal of what kind of contact the other couple must have had.

"How long were you with Alice?"

"It was only for a few seconds. Then I think the guy who's holding her came to the door, and the connection snapped off."

"If you could do it once, you can do it again."

"That's what I'm praying for," he answered. "I did try again. I got to the place, but I couldn't get through the door. I think I can't make contact with her unless she's receptive."

"You said—the guy who's holding her captive. What's his name?"

"Hayward."

"First or last?"

"She doesn't know."

"Well, maybe you can do some research."

"I'm planning on it."

He didn't add that he had to do *something* to keep from going insane until tonight.

CHAPTER EIGHT

For Jonah, getting through the day was like wading through thick mud where every step made you feel like you couldn't possibly go an inch farther.

His only option was to focus on Hayward, using every lead he could get on the Web. He found a town by that name. A county. Many people, including a professor at Johns Hopkins University. But an academic didn't seem like the right kind of guy.

Still he looked the prof up and determined that he was a very unlikely suspect.

The process was frustrating, particularly since Jonah didn't feel like he was doing anything besides eliminating leads. But it did keep his mind off contacting Alice. There was no use torturing himself by trying to do that until the two of them could have some quiet time.

～

Getting through the day was agony for Alice, especially since she sensed that Hayward was watching her every move more carefully than usual.

Finally, the exhausting physical routine was over, and she was alone in her cell again, eating her unexciting dinner. Still, she couldn't throw off the tension that seemed to weight her down like the blanket a dental technician used before X-raying your teeth. Moments after Jonah had flickered into existence in front of the door, Hayward had come bursting into the room. When Jonah came back, would they be interrupted again?

She didn't say "if." In her heart, she was determined it would be, "when."

After dinner, she forced herself to act as she normally did, taking a shower, putting on a nightgown, and climbing into bed.

When the lights dimmed, she breathed out a sigh of relief. Lying under the sheet and light blanket, she considered tactics. Should she try to make her mind blank? Or should she call out to Jonah and let him know she was waiting for him?

One thing she did understand—when he made it here, they must not talk out loud. Her exclamation was what had brought Hayward bursting into her cell this morning.

She closed her eyes, imagining the dark-haired man she had seen. When she could, she'd thought about him during the day. She guessed he was a little older than she was, but not much.

In her mind, she called out to him. *Jonah, I'm waiting for you. I'm trying to help you come here.* Then she couldn't stop herself from adding, *I need you.*

When she heard no answer, she felt a sharp pang. Still, she kept her gaze fixed on the spot by the door where he had appeared for a few seconds this morning. Did she see something flickering in the darkness? Or was that only what she was praying for?

To keep herself from speaking, she pressed her fingers to her mouth.

Jonah, she whispered in her mind. Had she really seen him for a few seconds this morning? She told herself it was true—and that Hayward had known it, too.

But that wasn't proof of anything. He'd only been reacting to *her* reaction.

She wasn't really expecting an answer when she called out again. But she heard him answer, *Yes.*

Thank God.

She kept her eyes focused on the place where she hoped he was standing. At first nothing changed. Then, all at once, she saw him, tall and broad shouldered. Well, he wasn't exactly there. He still looked like a ghost. She could see the door in back of him, through his body. Last time he'd been wearing only a pair of faded jeans, maybe because he thought he wasn't going to make it here. Now he had added a dark tee shirt.

He stood where he was for a long moment, looking around the cell.

This is where he keeps you?

Yes.

He made a rough sound. *The bastard.*

The way he said it sent a shiver along her nerve endings. She'd been thinking of Jonah as kind and gentle. Now she was seeing another side of him—the dangerous security agent.

It's okay, she said quickly.

The hell it is.

I've survived—so far.

Because you have grit.

Do I?

You must.

She liked hearing the way he talked about her, but words of praise would only stroke her ego—not free her. Changing the subject, she asked, *How did you get here?*

He looked like he was trying to figure out how to free her,

until he realized he wasn't going to fix anything immediately. *First I tried a self-hypnosis technique I've used before, and then I followed the sound of your "voice."*

Oh!

It was easier the second time. I guess I couldn't do it until we'd established a stronger connection.

How did you know to even try?

My friend Grant did it—with the woman who's his wife now. She was being held captive, too, and he was able to get there—and rescue her. Well, with help.

She swallowed hard, considering the implications.

He had been standing beside the door.

She held her breath as he crossed the room. It seemed to take forever. Then he was standing beside the bed. She could still partly see through him. But now he looked more solid.

Does he have a camera in here or something? Jonah asked.

I know he watches me. Not just here. In the other areas. So there must be a camera. Maybe they don't work with this low light.

She pushed off the bed, steadying herself before she took a step toward him. Then, before she could tell herself it was a bad idea, she reached around his body and clasped him in her arms. She hadn't even known if it was possible to hold onto him, but she felt his substance. When she closed her eyes to shut out his ghostly image, he felt even more solid and real. From his appearance, she had expected him to be cold—like a ghost. But he seemed to be the same temperature as the room.

She heard him make a small sound as she felt him circle her shoulders. His arms came up slowly, as though he had wondered the same thing as she about touching.

I can feel you, they both said at the same time.

Yes

Being clasped in his strong embrace was magic. And if she

kept her eyes closed, she could pretend he was well and truly here.

As she laid her head against his shoulder, he whispered in her mind, *I'm going to get you out of here.*

I know, she answered. And at that moment, against all odds, she believed him.

First, we have to figure out where you are.

Yes. She clung to him, swaying in his arms, marveling at how wonderful something so simple could be. She had had no normal human contact since Hayward had abducted her. This wasn't exactly normal, but it was a lot better than anything she had experienced with the monster who had brought her to this place.

Arthur Hayward had been fighting a sense of unease all day. For weeks he'd known that he had Alice totally under control. Then when he'd had lunch with her, he'd sensed a change. Until then, she'd always been totally deferential to him—as she should be. As he was holding forth on European history, he'd detected a note of hope in her eyes. The next day, when he'd brought her breakfast, she'd demonstrated a streak of defiance—as though she knew something important had changed.

But all that was nonsense, he assured himself, quickly. He'd captured and drugged her and totally covered his tracks with that gigantic rock fall out in the wilderness. No way could they bring in heavy equipment to move the rubble.

While the rescuers were scrambling around still hoping they could find her, he'd carried her to his car and driven away. Since then, he'd had total control over her every waking moment.

Still feeling unsettled, he got up from the comfortable wing-back chair in his office and strolled to the gun cabinet. After turning the key in the lock, he ran his fingers along the line of rifles. He loved Remingtons, Springfields, and Rugers. But his hand stopped when he came to the Mauser 98. German manufactured, it had been developed for military use, but it was just as good at stopping a charging lion—or a fleeing girl.

Paul Mauser's design was one of the best. Hayward took the beauty down from the rack, carried it to the chair and sat with the weapon on his lap, sliding his fingers along the stock and playing with the bolt action. As he caressed the rifle, he thought about what the gun could do to the woman in the basement. The best part was that she would think she had a chance to escape—which would give her courage. He imagined her stepping outside, dragging in a draft of the night air, and deciding which way she would run. And whichever way it was, he would follow.

He spent a very pleasant half hour imagining the scene—and her realization in the end that hope was a lie.

When he knew he was back in control of his emotions—and this whole situation, he got up to fix a cup of warm skimmed milk before he went to bed.

CHAPTER NINE

The sensation of Jonah's strong arms encircling Alice was intoxicating, but she needed more.

Still with her eyes closed, she raised her head, marveling that she could feel his breath on her face.

She wasn't sure who moved first, but all at once his lips were on hers. Maybe he had meant it to be a reassuring kiss. And at first she let it add to the perception of being safe in his arms. But too many emotions had been pent up inside her for too long. She'd been frightened. Despairing. Defiant. Resigned. But mostly she'd been so alone. Now a man who cared had come to rescue her. With all her heart, she wanted to believe that he could tip the balance of power with Hayward.

As he moved his lips against hers, she quickened to him on a primal level. All at once it was impossible for her to hold back a heated response to the light touch of his mouth on hers.

She sensed the urgency was the same for him. In the hours when they'd been apart, he must have spent a lot of time thinking about her. He could have walked away from a woman in distress, but he'd put forth an enormous effort to get here.

That knowledge helped fuel her need as he stroked his

hands up and down her back, then slid lower and cupped her bottom.

Glorying in his response to her, she opened her mouth for him, inviting even more intimacies.

Still with her eyes closed, she stroked her fingertips against his face, tracing his eyebrows, then the swirl of his ears. As their kisses turned hotter, she pressed her breasts against his chest and slid her hands down his back to his hips, trying to get as close to him as she could.

Her bed was only a few feet away, and she wanted to lie down with him. But when she took a step back, instead of following, he dropped his hands to his sides and stayed where he was. As her eyes blinked open she drew in a quick breath. After that heated exchange, she had expected to see him standing in front of her—a wholly solid figure. But he looked just as he had when he first appeared in her room.

I'm sorry. We have to stop, he whispered in her mind.

Why? Kissing him and stroking him, feeling his arms around her had been the first comfort she had experienced since she'd arrived in this awful place.

We have work to do. We have to figure out how to get you away from here.

In Jonah's arms, Alice had forgotten all about reality. But he was right, of course.

She swallowed hard, forcing herself not to reach for him again.

I'm going to see if I can find out anything useful.

How?

I'm not sure. What's outside the cell?

There's a hallway.

Right. When I came here that first time, I walked down it.

It leads to a gym and an exercise room. And there's a

stairway that goes up to the main part of the house. The door at the bottom is locked.

Okay.

As Jonah turned toward the door, he suppressed a surge of rage at the bastard who had done this to Alice—who was still doing it. The guy thought he knew how this drama was going to end, but Jonah was going for a surprise change in the rules.

He touched the door. He'd walked through it once. He could do it again, he told himself as he pressed his hand against the vertical surface. It felt solid, but it also felt spongy—as though he could feel through the molecules that made up its mass.

He rocked his hand, and to his satisfaction, he saw his fingers go through.

When he pressed forward, there was a feeling of resistance, and then he was on the other side and standing in the corridor he'd seen the night before.

The walls were made of gray-painted cinder blocks, like a school or other public building where cost cutting was a major consideration. In this case, the windowless hallway gave the feeling of being underground.

The floor under his feet was cheap tile. In fact, it looked like vinyl asbestos, which nobody used any more. That must mean it had been here for a while, or the guy didn't want to go to the expense of having asbestos abatement when it was removed.

There were light fixtures above him, each holding an old-fashioned low watt incandescent bulb—like the kind home improvement stores still sold in big packs. Each was enclosed by a wire cage which made it impossible to get to the fixtures.

He proceeded to his right. There were no doors immediately, but finally he came to an exercise room which seemed to be filled with standard equipment like a treadmill, a bike and racks of weights, all outdated models.

A little farther on was a larger gym, big enough for a basketball court. Ropes dangled from the ceiling along one wall. Another wall had netting like you might see on a military obstacle course.

He exited the gym and walked toward another door. It had a window, and when he saw a flight of stairs that led up, he felt his heart start to pound. At the top, he could get outside and find out where he was.

But when he pressed his hand against the door the way he'd done in Alice's cell, nothing happened. It remained a solid barrier, and he couldn't do the trick of pushing through.

He cursed silently. Probably he was at the limit of his range. He'd opened himself to Alice and used her to draw him here. She must be the key to how far he could go. With a grimace he turned and walked back down the hall.

When Jonah disappeared, Alice felt a terrible sense of loss. She backed up and sat on the bed, staring at the spot where he had disappeared, wondering how long he would be gone and if he would return. As she sat with her pulse pounding, she wasn't sure what to hope for.

Seconds ticked by. Then minutes. Had the connection to him been cut again?

She had almost given up hope, when she saw the wall waver, and suddenly he was back in the room.

What happened? She asked.

I was in the corridor that led to the gym and the exercise room. I saw the door to the stairs, but I couldn't get any farther.

She heard the frustration suffusing his inner voice.

Why not?

I think it has something to do with being close to you. I can only get a certain distance away from you.

Disappointment made her fists clench. She'd hoped he'd be able to get out of the house—or at least upstairs.

I couldn't see outside, so I don't know where we are.

Not your fault.

We have to try something else.

What?

I don't know. He sounded discouraged, and she fought her own disappointment. Just his coming here had felt like a miracle. And it was. But it wasn't enough to save her life. The longer she was trapped in this place, the less likely she was to get out alive.

He had remained near the door.

Stepping across the small room, she pressed against him, and his arms came up to encircle her.

He stroked his hands up and down her back, and his touch sent little currents of electricity over her skin. *I'm not sure what's best,* he murmured inside her mind.

In what way?

Since this is—paranormal—there are a lot of ways to think about it. If I build up the connection with you, maybe I can get upstairs. On the other hand, what if I get more substantial? I can already touch you. Any more substance, and I might not be able to get through the door. But being more here might mean I could stop him from hurting you.

She hadn't considered any of that.

You're right. There are a lot of ways to think about it. But I vote for the idea of us getting closer.

Let's see what happens if you focus on me.

She liked that suggestion. Closing her eyes, she clasped her hands around Jonah's head and brought his mouth to hers. She felt a moment of resistance before he gave himself over to her.

She felt a flare of triumph as he moved his lips against hers, sliding, nibbling, and then urging her to open for him. When she did, his tongue slipped into her mouth, and she gloried in the intimacy of the kiss.

Without letting go of him, she moved backwards until she felt the bed frame hit her lower legs. Bending her knees, she sat down, bringing him with her.

It was hard to keep her eyes closed. She longed to look at him, but she knew that if she did, it would break the magic spell that fate had woven around them.

Alice. His inner voice sounded gritty as he said her name.

I want to forget about this place. You're the only one who can carry me away.

I know.

She had been as direct as she could be, but she couldn't say more. She rolled to her side, still kissing him.

One of his hands combed through her hair. The other stroked the side of her breast, and she knew he was asking permission to go farther.

Yes.

He shifted so he could cup both her breasts, gently kneading and caressing her through the thin fabric of her gown. She arched into the wonderful sensations he was creating as he squeezed and shaped her. Her nipples had contracted to tight points, and when he played with them through her gown, she couldn't hold back a gasp.

You like that?

Lord, yes. She didn't have a lot of experience with men, but no one had ever made her feel like this. She longed to open her eyes and watch what he was doing to her, but she knew that would only interfere with his wonderful fantasy. She thought about pulling off her gown. But she was too shy for that. Instead, she lay back, giving him as much access to her body as she could.

She sensed him leaning over her. One hand stayed on her breast. With the other, he reached to play with her toes. She had never thought of that as erotic, but it was with him.

He stroked her ankles, then her calves before dabbling with the edge of her gown. When she didn't tell him to stop, he moved upward, caressing her knee, sending hot sensations curling toward her center. He followed them to her thigh, first the outside curve and then the sensitive interior skin.

Okay?

"Yes."

In response, he worked his way higher, moving slowly, and she knew he was silently asking permission again, this time to touch her intimately.

Yes

He cupped her sex, pressing against her. When she arched into the caress, he responded with a firmer touch, rocking the heel of his hand against her. And as her breathing accelerated, he parted her lips so that he could glide into her slick folds.

She had never gone this far with a man before. When the intimacy made her jump, he immediately pulled his hand back.

I shouldn't have done that.

It's what I want. "Don't stop." She whispered the last part aloud.

Are you sure?

Yes.

When he gently repeated the caress, she marveled at how well he could do this. He seemed to know exactly how to kindle her pleasure.

He dipped into her vagina, just the barest bit, twisting his finger, the sensations exquisite.

As he withdrew, she made a pleading sound. But he wasn't

going far. As he stroked and pressed, her total focus was on the sensual pleasure he was creating. She knew he was gauging her reactions, finding out what she liked best.

She gripped his shoulders, letting his sorcery enfold her. As he took her up and up, she moved her hips against his hand, increasing the friction, silently begging him to take her over the edge.

Her breath came in gasps as he lifted her up to a high plane where there was only heat and light—stoking the flames until they burst through her in a glorious spasm.

Afterwards, as she lay limp with satisfaction, his lips brushed her cheek.

That was selfish of me.

No. I loved watching your pleasure.

That made her cheeks heat.

I'm shameless.

Of course not.

As he silently spoke the words, she heard a noise in the hall.

Oh no.

Jonah moved away from her just as she heard the lock turn. Her eyes flew open, and with a shaky hand, she pushed herself up, leaning back against the wall just as the door opened.

She knew her face was still hot, her breathing ragged.

The light in the cell had been dim. As it flashed to brightness, she lifted her arm to shield her eyes. But she could see a pair of men's legs standing in the doorway. Hayward. Who else would it be? Moving her arm a little, she saw he was holding a gun, the way he had last time she'd seen him.

"What the hell is going on here?" he demanded, his fiery gaze searing her.

She shook her head. "Nothing's going on," she protested, her voice quavery.

"You're moving around. Talking to someone."

"Maybe I'm finally going crazy," she answered, repeating what she had said the last time he'd questioned her.

"Yeah, maybe."

She used the light as an excuse to shield her face, but she knew Jonah had gotten up and moved away from her. He had seemed to flicker out of existence when Hayward had opened the door. Now his image steadied as he walked to the side, where he had a line of sight to her captor.

Her gaze swung back to the man with the gun. She had always figured the way to stay alive here was to be compliant. Perhaps that was no longer true. And perhaps she could give the man who thought he had the upper hand something to worry about.

"Is this place haunted?" she asked, putting a shiver into her voice.

Both men in the room looked startled. Hayward recovered and gave her a hard look. "Not that I know of. Why?"

"You asked if I was talking to someone. I think I saw a ghost."

He laughed, although she could hear a little waver in the sound. "That's ridiculous."

Jonah apparently liked her inspiration. He stepped toward Hayward and waved his hand in front of the man's face.

Hayward made a low sound and took a quick step back. "What was that?"

"I don't know. Did you see something?"

"You didn't?"

"No."

He punched out his next words as he said, "You're the one who mentioned ghosts."

"Because I think there's one down here."

His voice was icy now. "What did you see exactly?"

"A flickering in the air in the room."

As she spoke, Jonah waved his hand again, and Hayward moved quickly to the side. The gun in his hand swung toward Jonah, and she gasped.

"What?"

"Nothing."

The gun swung back to her. "Don't tell me nothing."

Apparently he can see something, Jonah said. *But he can't hurt me.*

You think.

She raised her chin. "Does it feel suddenly colder in here?" she asked.

"No," Hayward shot back, then looked around again. "I've never seen a ghost here."

"Maybe it's the spirit of a slave who died on this plantation."

He looked uncertain. "What makes you say it's a plantation?"

"The house looks like it. It's old. Big. Opulent."

"Okay." He stopped short as though he thought he'd given something away.

"Maryland was a slave state," she said, watching him carefully. He didn't deny they were still in Maryland, but he didn't confirm it, either.

"Is the ghost a man or a woman?" Hayward asked.

"A man."

"Did he look like a slave?"

"I don't know. I couldn't see him clearly. I felt the temperature in the room change and saw flickering."

He made a dismissive sound. "I think you're putting me on."

"How could I?"

"By pretending something's going on that isn't."

"I'm not pretending anything," she protested. "And you're the one who came charging in here because you said you heard me with someone."

Anger flashed in his eyes, but he didn't speak.

A few feet away, she saw Jonah move again. He drew back his foot and kicked out, striking at Hayward's legs.

The kidnapper made a squeaking sound. "What was that?"

"What?"

He took a step back, torn between anger and fear. "You did something."

She spread her hands. "No. How could I?"

"I don't know."

"I think this calls for an evaluation of the whole situation."

"What do you mean?"

"I think we're going to have to move things along a little faster."

"What?"

"You're causing problems, and I'm tired of dealing with you."

She stared at him in shock as he backed out of the room. The door slammed, and she was alone with the supposed ghost.

What did he mean by that? Jonah asked.

Her mouth was so dry she could barely answer. Luckily she didn't have to speak to say, *I guess he means we're going to have the hunt—soon.*

CHAPTER TEN

Shit.

Jonah stared from Alice to the closed door and back again. He'd known she was in serious trouble. He hadn't realized the living hell of her situation until he'd seen her captor in action.

Fury consumed him. He wanted to stride across the room to Alice and wrap his arms protectively around her. That would only be temporary comfort, but maybe the bastard had given him an opportunity.

Be right back, he shouted in his mind as he pushed through the door, watching the man's rigid back as he stomped down the hall.

Jonah ran after him. When he caught up, he aimed a kick at the guy's ass.

Hayward cried out and whirled, looking wildly around. He seemed to focus on Jonah, and he gasped. For a charged moment, the two men might have been staring at each other. Then Hayward shook his head, and his gaze flicked away. Before the man could turn around, Jonah kicked him in the shin.

"Jesus," he howled.

"You miserable coward," Jonah shouted. "You're afraid to pick on someone your own size, so you have to bully a girl."

"What the hell is going on here?" Hayward bellowed.

"Wouldn't you like to know?"

Had the man actually heard that? Jonah couldn't be sure.

Hayward pointed the gun at Jonah.

"Go ahead."

For a moment Jonah thought he was going to shoot. Then he seemed to pull himself together. Turning, he walked down the hall, his shoulders rigid. When he reached the stairs, Jonah stayed close.

Hayward unlocked the door and stepped through.

A few minutes ago Jonah hadn't been able to get out of the basement. To his relief, he could step through after the kidnapper. It seemed he had established a strong enough connection with the man to follow him. Unwilling to lose that advantage, Jonah stuck with the owner of the house as he walked to the floor above.

Hoping against hope that this would give him the information he needed, Jonah kept pace, although he wasn't sure why he could do it. They walked into a formal dining room furnished in an antique style. But instead of having one large table in the middle, it was divided into two separate areas by a mesh grill. Each side of the grill had a square table, one about the size of a card table and the other a little larger. It was the room Alice had described. Jonah saw that between the heavy drapes, the windows were covered with sheets of wood.

The owner of the house stepped through a gate at the left side of the grill, then exited into a butler's pantry which led to a large kitchen. It was mansion sized, but it looked like it hadn't been remodeled since the fifties. The top of the white refrigerator was rounded. The stove was an outdated electric model, the countertop looked like marble laminate, and the cabinets were white metal.

Hayward opened one and pulled out a bottle of vintage Scotch and a glass. He poured himself a generous draft of the amber liquid and downed it in a couple of swallows. Then he stood, breathing hard.

Jonah studied the killer's pinched expression. The guy was seriously spooked by his encounter with the ghost. Hopefully that was good. But now Jonah knew it was also very dangerous for Alice.

Desperate for more information, Jonah looked around the kitchen. In one corner he saw a calendar tacked to the wall. He tried to get closer, but he couldn't move far from Hayward.

Squinting, he struggled to make out details. He could see the month, but not the year. Then his heart clunked when he read the words Carvertown Business Association.

Carvertown. That was on Maryland's Eastern Shore. Wasn't Rouse College there?

My God, could this be the location where Alice was being held?

It was almost too good to be true. Yet why else would Alice's captor have the calendar on his wall. Once again, Jonah tried to step away from the man so that he could go exploring on his own, but when he got more than a few feet, he felt his hold on the scene slipping as it had before.

With a silent curse, he went back, hovering over Hayward. The bastard put the empty glass down with a thunk on the counter, then walked toward another door. Jonah shadowed him, praying he wasn't going to evaporate before he found out what he needed to know.

Gray light was coming through the window, and Jonah realized he'd been here all night.

Hayward walked down a short hall and into a library with a

comfortable leather sofa and chairs grouped around a fireplace and shelves of books on two sides of the room. On a stand by the desk was a rack with pipes.

Behind the desk was a gun cabinet with a collection of hunting rifles.

Jonah drew in a quick breath. Maybe the guy practiced on deer, but he'd made it clear they wasn't his prey this time.

Hayward opened the cabinet, took out one of the weapons and examined it, testing the action. Then he put it back with a satisfied look on his face. Jonah wanted to smack him in the mouth, but thought it wouldn't be a good idea now.

Instead, he dragged his eyes away from the sick bastard and looked toward the windows.

Unlike in the dining room, there was a view outside, and in the early morning light, Jonah saw a spacious green lawn and a formal garden with many paths and hedges. In one direction was a woods and in the other was a river. In the middle of the water was a rock formation that looked like an enormous upside down boot.

"Bingo," he muttered as he stared at it. There couldn't be another boulder like that in the area, could there?

He wanted to rush back downstairs and give Alice the good news that he thought he knew where to find her. But when he tried to move away from Hayward, he had the same problem as before. He was glued to the man.

"Shit."

Alice. Alice, can you hear me? He tried to call to her, but there was no answer. He could only think that too much had happened for them to connect now. Again he cursed.

He wanted to stay here until he could reach her. Maybe Hayward would even go downstairs again, and Jonah could follow. But he knew that hanging around would be dangerous. The hunt could be only hours away. He had to get back to

Decorah, make sure he knew where this place was, and plan the rescue mission.

Yet when he tried to send his mind back to where he lay in his bed, he couldn't move.

Clenching his fists, he put more effort into tearing himself away. Nothing changed.

He wanted to scream in frustration. Instead he closed his eyes, blotting out the scene around him, imagining himself back in his bed. Every fiber of his being clenched as he tried to break away. Eons passed, and he knew he hadn't moved.

"Come on, come on," he railed, straining against the invisible bonds that held him here.

He might have given up and relaxed for a few minutes, but getting back was too important. Finally, finally it worked, and he felt like he'd been caught in a strong wind.

It swept him away, and he landed with a thump on his bed, gasping for breath.

Sweat poured off his body. When he tried to get up, his head spun. Although he wanted to rush to the laptop sitting on his desk, he knew he had to give himself a few minutes.

He pressed the back of his head into the pillow, struggling to control his breathing. When he couldn't wait any longer, he pushed himself up and lurched across the room, grasping the back of the chair when he reached the desk.

Still shaky he lowered himself to the seat. He wanted to stagger to the bathroom and get a drink of water, but this was more important.

He got into Google and called up information on the Carver River. It had several unusual rock formations, and a famous one shaped like an upside down boot was at a bend of the river. The photographs were of the rock he'd seen. But the only Google Earth pictures were blurred satellite images. There were no "street scenes" along the river.

He glanced at his watch. Although it was only 6:30 in the morning, this could be the day of the hunt, judging from what Hayward had said. Well, more likely the night of the hunt, when the bastard would have the cover of darkness.

It would get dark around 6:30pm. That gave Jonah all day to organize a rescue operation and get down there.

Knowing he'd be waking Grant, he called the other Decorah agent.

"What's up?" his friend asked, sounding remarkably alert.

"I think I've pinpointed Alice's location."

"Where is she?"

"Carvertown. At a big estate on the Carver River."

"How do you know?"

"I managed to get to the place—like you did when you got to Jenny. Then I was able to follow the guy named Hayward upstairs. First I saw a calendar from the Carvertown Business Association in the kitchen. Then I looked out the window and saw the river and a distinctive rock. When I Googled that, I could see where the estate was on the river. I tried to get back to Alice and tell her, but I couldn't do it. And after that, I had a hell of a time even getting back here." He stopped and took a breath before starting again.

"I want to plan a rescue mission, but I also want to verify the location as soon as possible. Hayward, the guy who is holding her captive was pretty angry. I think he could be moving up his hunt to tonight."

"Okay, got it."

"How soon can you meet me at the helo pad?"

"I can be there in half an hour. But won't Hayward wonder why somebody's flying over? Wouldn't a drone be better?"

"We'll make it quick. I want to see it for myself." He heard the urgency in his own voice.

"You're sure of the location?"

"No. But I'm sure that rock will clue me in when we get to the river." He wanted to shout at his friend to stop asking questions, but he knew they were legitimate.

When Grant finally said, "Okay," Jonah breathed out a sigh.

Thankful that his friend hadn't put up any objections, Jonah dressed in record time and was at the Decorah helipad ten minutes early.

Both men were rated for flying the machine, but Jonah told Grant to climb in the pilot's seat because he wanted to pay attention to the location.

Jonah showed Grant a picture of the rock he'd downloaded. Then, using the GPS, they plotted a course.

After they crossed the Chesapeake Bay, Jonah kept his gaze trained out the window.

"There's the river," he told Grant as they approached Carvertown.

"What do you want me to do?"

"Follow it until we see the rock."

They flew along the river, with Jonah glued to the window. Finally he spotted the formation in the distance. Grant saw it too and headed straight for it.

Jonah could see the estate along the left-hand bank. But something was wrong. He blinked as he studied the house.

The hairs on the back of his neck prickled when he saw it was a blackened, burned-out hulk.

CHAPTER ELEVEN

"We're too late," Jonah gasped, feeling his heart turn over as he stared down. "He burned the place."

As he dug his nails into the edge of his seat, he saw Grant follow his gaze, then bank and circle. He came down for a landing near the house and a sign that said, "No Trespassing. Danger. Keep Out." Jonah scrambled out and ran toward the ruined building.

Grant cut the engine and followed.

Jonah struggled to stop himself from howling as he stared at the burned structure. Examining the contours of the building, he could make out a wing below ground, where he saw a room big enough to be a gym. Leading to it must be the corridor with Alice's cell. In the other direction was the stairway to the main part of the house. He thought he saw the dining room, then the kitchen.

"My God, what happened?" he gasped out.

"You're sure this is the right place?" Grant asked.

Jonah's mouth was so parched he could hardly speak, but he managed to say, "It's the layout."

Grant cleared his throat. "But this isn't a new fire."

"What?"

"You're saying you left this morning. This place was burned a long time ago."

Jonah tried to drag air into his lungs as he struggled to digest what his friend was saying. "A long time ago," he repeated.

Grant gestured toward the faded sign. "That's not new either."

"Jesus," was all Jonah could say as he tried to cope with what he was seeing and what it meant.

"Let's go back to how Alice contacted you," Grant said in a steady voice.

"On the radio of the 1955 Chevy I was restoring."

"Yeah." His friend let that hang in the air between them.

"1955," Jonah repeated, as other details leaped into his mind. The floor in the prison had been vinyl asbestos—a material that was no longer used. The kitchen had looked antique. And then there was the way he'd drawn a blank when he'd tried to find someone named Alice Davenport. It had seemed as if she hadn't existed. "My God—is it possible—do you think I've been communicating with someone who's in 1955?"

"Yeah," Grant answered. Probably only another Decorah agent would have agreed with Jonah's assessment. But they'd all been through too many weird things to discount what would seem impossible to a layman. Plus, Grant had psychic powers that were similar to Jonah's.

The enormity of the realization rolled over him as though he'd been flattened by a steamroller. "Then it's already too late," he gasped out.

"No."

"Hayward already hunted and killed her."

Grant clasped Jonah by the shoulders and shook him. "You're not thinking straight," he bellowed. "You talked to her.

Then you told me you went back there. She was alive when you were there."

Jonah tried to grasp on to that like a drowning man who had snatched at a log floating by.

"I'd better ask you—the time of day was the same, right?"

"What do you mean?"

"You got there at night, when she was in her cell."

"Yes."

"Then it's the same time there now. If he's going to hunt her tonight, you've got plenty of time to get there."

"I was going to bring a bunch of Decorah agents to screw up Hayward's plans."

"I guess you're gonna have to do it by yourself," Grant said.

"Christ. I wasn't even there. Not the solid me, I mean. I was like a ghost."

"I started out like that when I first got to where Jenny was being held," Grant said. "If I can do it, you can too."

"Maybe," Jonah conceded.

"The first thing we'd better do is consult Frank and get organized."

"But you can't come back with me."

"Maybe there's something we can do."

The sound of an engine made them both turn to see a police car coming up the road.

"Oh shit," Jonah muttered as he remembered the "No Trespassing" sign.

A middle-aged cop in a tan uniform got out and walked toward them. His body was going to fat, and he scowled as he looked from the two Decorah agents to the helicopter and back again.

"This is private property." His burnished name tag said "Cooper."

"Sorry officer."

"What are you doing here?"

"Looking for a kidnap victim," Jonah said. "We're agents with Decorah Security in Beltsville. We've both got creds. I'm going to reach into my pocket and get mine."

Cooper watched him produce his wallet and flip it open to his Decorah ID card, then nodded.

"Jonah Ranger?"

"Yes."

"And who are you?" he asked Grant, who also produced his ID

When they'd verified their identities, the cop said. "We haven't gotten any word of a kidnapping."

"The family is keeping it quiet," Jonah answered, wondering how big a hole he was digging himself into.

"Well, as you can see, nobody's here," he cop said.

"Okay, I guess our tip didn't pan out," Grant said, then added, "When did this place burn down?"

"1961."

The two Decorah agents exchanged glances.

"Do you know how the fire started?"

"No." Cooper gave them a long look. "Why so many questions?"

"Because from the tip we got, we expected to find someone living here," Jonah answered.

"Well, you got lousy information."

"Seems like it." Jonah cleared his throat, then asked, "And the place had been a burned out shell all this time?"

"There was some question whether Arthur Hayward died in the fire. Then the Hayward family sued the crap out of each other to get the property. It's still in litigation."

"Anybody ever look for unmarked graves around the estate?" Jonah asked.

The cop's head snapped toward him. "What?"

"Arthur Hayward may have killed some women."

"That was a long time ago."

"They're still dead. Maybe you want to go through your cold cases."

Cooper's eyes narrowed. "First you say you're looking for a kidnap victim. Then you claim there are bodies buried here."

"I can't change what we've been told," Jonah said, but he figured he'd better not press his luck. He and Grant return to the helo.

When they had taken off and put their headsets back on, Jonah looked out the window toward the house and snapped several pictures.

Through his microphone, he said, "The fire was 1961, not 1955."

"But I guess the car was still being driven back then," Grant said. "It's still drivable, right?"

"Because I worked on it." Switching subjects, Jonah said, "She told me his name was Hayward."

"Yeah."

"Now we've got his first name. We can do some research when we get back."

"I want to be here!"

"I know, but you came to the estate in the past while you were lying in your bed. That's probably your best strategy."

"I don't know. I lost contact with her before I left."

"You just need to relax and reach out to her—like you did before."

Jonah gave his friend a long look. He knew Grant was trying to reassure him, but he wasn't going to be reassured until he got back here—in 1961. He swore again under his breath. To say this was weird would be the understatement of the century.

"I'm coming back in the car," he said.

"What?"

"I'm driving the car down here. The car radio was my first point of contact with Alice. I'll park it in the woods and go from there."

"You're not being rational."

"Were you rational when you thought you'd lost Jenny?"

"You have a point."

"Plus, if I get her out of there, I can bring her back and drive home in the car." He hated the word "if." "No—*when* I get her out of there," he corrected.

Luckily Grant didn't ask how he was going to bring Alice to this time period—because Jonah would have screamed that he didn't know.

As they flew, he got out his cell phone and looked up Arthur Hayward on the Web. Apparently the man had inherited wealth and had always felt entitled to live outside the rules of ordinary men. He had been a famous big game hunter in the fifties and had retired to his family estate where he led a reclusive life. The articles didn't say he'd also become a very effective serial killer, although it did say his wife had died when she'd gone on a hunting trip to Africa with him. Yeah, sure. Probably he'd arranged her death—his first kill.

"You find anything that can help Alice?" Grant asked.

"No. Only confirmation that the house did burn down in 1961, and the guy was a first-class bastard."

CHAPTER TWELVE

"We're having the hunt tonight," Hayward said as he brought Alice her breakfast.

She'd been expecting that news. Still she felt a chill sweep over her skin as the words echoed through her cell.

There was more food on her breakfast tray than usual. The condemned woman eats a hearty breakfast, she thought as she stared at the greasy eggs and bacon, along with hashed browns and toast. Too bad she had very little appetite. But she forced herself to choke down some of the food because she knew she was going to need her strength for the ordeal to come.

As she ate, she tried to contact Jonah, but he didn't answer, and she felt like the two of them were suddenly living on different planets. And how could he help her anyway? He had barely been able to get Hayward's attention, and the result was the opposite of what she'd hoped. He'd managed to scare her captor into moving up her execution date.

When she'd finished eating, the slot in the door opened again, and a set of clothing came through the door. There was a pair of comfortable dark pants, a long-sleeved dark shirt, dark socks and dark tennis shoes. She'd been afraid he was going to make her wear white so that she would be more visible. These clothes would give her some protection—unless there were hidden glow-in-the-dark patches that she couldn't see.

"Get dressed," he told her as he delivered the clothing. "Then we're going upstairs."

Almost as soon as she was dressed, the door opened again.

"Go up," Hayward's voice boomed from a hidden speaker.

Wishing her pulse would stop pounding, she followed the corridor to the stairs, then up. The door to the dining room was closed, and her only option was a side passage, which she took with some trepidation.

Suppose he was trying to fool her, and the hunt was going to begin now?

She walked cautiously, but there were no tricks waiting in the corridor, which led her to a wood-paneled room that was designed to be a library or a den. Like the dining room, it was nicely furnished with polished wood antique pieces. There was a sofa, comfortable chairs and a desk. But she almost winced when she saw the gun cabinet against the wall. Hayward, who was watching carefully for her reaction, grinned.

"The rifles are for later," he said in a cheerful tone as he pulled a pistol from the middle desk drawer and put it near himself on the desktop. "Right now, it's time for a picture-taking session." He picked up what she recognized as a Polaroid camera. "Stand over there by the bookshelf," he said.

She moved near the shelves, her eyes darting to the side table where a rack of pipes sat. Her breath caught when she saw a pack of matches lying on the table beside the rack.

Hayward looked down to fiddle with the camera. In that quick moment, she snaked out her hand, picked up the matches and thrust them into her pocket.

When he looked up and scowled, she thought he'd seen the theft. But he was concerned with her stance.

"Take your hand out of your pocket," he snapped. "Stand up straight the way I taught you. And face me."

Her heart was drumming as she followed his directions, lifting her chin and trying to look defiant as he pushed the shutter.

Again he looked at the camera and clicked the shutter. She wasn't sure how long it took to develop the picture, but finally a square of photographic paper came out of the front of the camera. Hayward held it up. At first there was only a blur of black and white. Then the image began to emerge. As she watched, she saw herself standing by the shelves.

"I like your spirit," he said as he looked at the picture, then waved it in the air to dry it. "I do like to have a good record of my guests. Let's have one more."

His guests. She supposed he meant the women he had killed.

He snapped another photo and waited for the picture to reveal itself once more.

"I think the first one is better," he mused as he compared the two.

She shrugged, wondering if this performance was designed to unnerve her. If so, it was working.

"Have a seat," he said, indicating the guest chair on her side of the desk.

He sat as well, putting down the camera and the developed photos and picking up the gun.

"Just a precaution," he said as he pointed the revolver at her. "I don't want you to get any ideas about attacking me."

In truth, she'd been wondering if she could lunge across the desk and knock him over. She was stronger now than she ever had been in her life, and maybe she could have inflicted some damage on him. Maybe she could even have gotten away, but not now with him holding a gun so close to her.

A manila folder lay in the center of the desk blotter, and he pushed it toward her.

"Inside are photographs of the grounds. Plus maps. You can take them back to your room and study them until it's time for us to meet again."

She reached for the folder and started to open it.

"Save it until you get downstairs. I don't want to have to sit here babysitting you."

She answered with a small nod as she clenched her fingers around the edge of the folder.

"Everything you need is in there. Give yourself ample time to study the layout of the estate."

Yeah, sure, she thought. Everything she needed except what would make it a fair fight—like he'd have weapons and she wouldn't. But he was setting the rules, and this was going to be as good as she got.

"It's all outdoors?"

"Yes."

"What time are we doing it?" she asked.

"Around seven. It will be fully dark by then." It was obvious he was enjoying this conversation. He was the mastermind who was finally going to reap the fruits of all his hard work. Or rather, her hard work.

She flipped quickly through the folder, just trying to get a general impression of the playing field. "And this is really what the grounds look like?"

His eyes flashed. "I'm not going to trick you. Like you did with that ghost crap last night."

His anger and the words made her stomach knot. She wanted to say there might be a ghost to surprise him. But she couldn't be sure Jonah would show up to help her.

"It wasn't crap," she answered, like they were having a

discussion about a sporting match. Well, for him it probably was. For her, it was life and death.

"Where's your ghost now?"

She shrugged. "I don't control him. Ghosts come and go as they please."

He laughed. "Right."

She gestured toward her outfit, with the matches in the pants pocket. "This is what I'm wearing?" She held her breath as she waited for the answer.

"Yes."

"Why black?"

"I like the challenge."

"What if I just lie down in the woods and don't move?"

"I'll get you in the morning. And I'll use a knife—not a gun."

She fought a zing of sickness.

"You should go do your homework."

While Jonah was looking up Hayward, Grant contacted Decorah and explained the situation. By the time they arrived back at headquarters, Frank and a group of agents were waiting for them.

"So your rescue mission is complicated by time travel," Frank said when they were all seated in the conference room.

Apparently he'd filled everyone in on the situation because nobody looked shocked—only impressed that Jonah had made a connection with a kidnap victim across such a terrible divide.

"I'm driving down there in the car," Jonah said. "It was the initial link between us."

Frank nodded. "And you think of it as a good luck charm."

"Right."

"Then what?"

"Then I don't know. I hope I can get back to Alice again."

"When was the last time you contacted her?"

"Last night. After that, some stuff happened with the kidnapper, and we didn't hook up again."

"Have you tried since?"

"Yes."

The admission hung in the air.

"I'm hoping it will be easier once I get to Carvertown."

Grant told them about the hostile cop showing up. "Jonah won't be able to drive onto the estate."

"I'll park as close as possible. Or maybe if I come in a car instead of a helo, nobody will notice."

"Except that they may be on the lookout for you."

"Unfortunately."

"You could take a werewolf with you to keep the cop occupied," Cole Marshall said.

Jonah shook his head. "He'd probably shoot you."

When the meeting broke up, Frank asked Jonah to stay behind. "Are you emotionally involved with her?"

"I don't know her all that well."

"But how do you feel about her?" Frank pressed.

"I want desperately to save her," he admitted in a low voice.

"Then focus on your emotions when you try to connect with her again," he said.

"Why?"

"Just a hunch I have."

Alice stood, goose bumps rising on her arms as she turned away from her captor. She knew he had been toying with her—deliberately stoking her fears. She felt hardly any better when she left the room, taking the side passage and making her way back downstairs to the familiar corridor that led to the cell where she'd lived for the past . . ." She stopped. Well, at least two months according to what Jonah had told her. Sometimes it felt like years and sometimes it felt like the last days of her life had gone by in a flash.

She stepped into the cell but didn't bother to close the door, sure that he had locked her back into the lower level of the house. As she stood in the center of the room, she wanted to thrust her hand into her pocket and make sure the matches were still there. But that might be a dead giveaway that she had stolen something useful. Instead, she sat down on the bed and opened the folder.

The first thing she saw was a picture of a grand mansion house in the red brick Georgian style with a portico entrance held up by white Doric columns. The next photo pulled back from the house so she could see gravel paths that ran through formal gardens. Another picture must have been taken from the roof of the mansion. It showed more of the garden layout, plus a maze made of manicured hedges. There were additional pictures of woods and vast fields. Her heart leaped when she saw a river in the background. If she could get to it, could she dive in and swim to safety? It looked promising, but there must be a catch. Maybe he'd salted the shoreline with land mines—or sharp stakes. It couldn't be easy to get away by water.

If there were sharp stakes could she pull one up and use it to attack Hayward? Yeah, and how would she even get close to him?

She knew that her captor was playing a psychological game with her. He wanted her on edge. He wanted her to make the wrong decisions tonight. Too bad she didn't know what was best. Maybe she'd have a better idea when she could see the grounds in person.

She focused on the material in the folder for as long as she could. Hayward brought a lunch tray. Weirdly, it was fried chicken and mashed potatoes, things he hadn't permitted during her stay here. Under other circumstances, she might have enjoyed them, but that was impossible today. She ate a little because she knew she would need fuel.

And she would also need to be rested, she told herself. Lying down, she closed her eyes and tried to relax. When she couldn't turn her mind off, she tried to reach out to Jonah. She'd never contacted him during the day, and she had the feeling it wasn't going to work, but she sent her mind out to him anyway.

Jonah, Hayward is having the hunt tonight. I have a surprise for him, but I need your help. Where are you? Please come back to me.

She repeated the message as she had done the first night she'd contacted him, praying that he would hear her. He didn't answer, but she couldn't stop clinging to the feeling that he was nearby. Maybe closer than he ever had been.

Still he didn't answer, and she decided that was just wishful thinking. Closing her eyes, she ordered herself to relax on the narrow bed. Somehow, against all odds, she did slip into sleep.

CHAPTER THIRTEEN

Jonah had dressed in dark jeans, shirt, jacket and running shoes. His Sig was in a shoulder holster under his jacket. He probably couldn't shoot Hayward, but having the weapon made him feel better.

He arrived in Carvertown around 5:00pm wishing it weren't still full daylight as he headed toward the Hayward estate in the bright turquoise boat of a Chevy that stuck out among all the modern cars. He passed the entrance, a weed-choked lane that had probably once been paved, and drove farther down the road, looking for a good place to park. He didn't have to go far to find a small wooded area. Pulling the car under the trees, he cut the engine and sat for a minute with his hands clenching the steering wheel.

Frank had told him to focus on his emotions, and that wasn't going to be a problem. All his hopes and fears for the evening churned inside him like an interior hurricane.

He reached for the knob on the radio, then pulled his hand back. Alice might be busy getting ready, and he didn't want to break her concentration as she prepared for her ordeal.

Tension buzzed through him, partly because he had no idea

whether he could actually get back to Alice. Finding out that she was living in an era before he was born had been a horrible shock. Had the shock been so great that it would keep him from traveling there again?

It was hard to stay in the car. He wanted to get up and *do* something—if only it was to pace through the woods. But because he knew it was better to stay out of sight, he forced himself to sit still for another twenty minutes.

Then his nerves simply wouldn't let him remain idle. What if he waited too long and it was too late?

When he couldn't stand the tension any longer, he got out and stretched before heading across the fields toward the burned-out ruin of the mansion, his eyes alert for any sign of the cop who had questioned him and Grant that morning.

He'd spent the afternoon looking at the aerial photos he'd taken of the estate. He was pretty sure he knew the layout of the place. And probably it hadn't changed much, thanks to the family dispute that kept the property from being developed. The grounds were overgrown. Doubtless the exterior had been better taken care of in Hayward's time. But he kept his eye out for places where Alice could hide if she needed to.

It was getting dark when he found some cover in a small stand of saplings. Still he waited with his eyes closed, praying he could get back to Alice. It might be harder now because he understood the distance between them. But he wasn't going to let that stop him.

Instead, he pictured her and did what Frank had advised. He let his emotions bloom, let his longing to be with Alice guide him to her—past all the years between them.

At first it didn't work, and he felt panic start to swallow him whole. Then he ordered himself to calm down.

"Steady," he muttered. "Steady. You've done this before.

You can do it again. You did it when you didn't know the time difference. You can still do it."

Yet he understood it didn't matter what he told himself. Learning how far away she really was had given him a bad shock.

Arthur Hayward sat in his comfortable library drumming his fingers on the desktop. He was impatient for the hunt. Yet he couldn't start until dark, lest a passing boater on the river could see what was going on at the estate.

He stood up, poured a finger of Scotch and downed it in one swallow. His nerves were so raw that he had to force himself not to ring the gong that signaled the start of the game. He'd had Alice Davenport under strict control—like the other women he'd taken. Now the bitch was ruining his pleasure. Something had happened, something he couldn't understand, and all he wanted to do was get rid of the little cunt.

Previously, he'd drawn out the hunt. He'd let his prey think she had a chance to get away, and he'd watched her circle around the grounds, trying to find a way out. Not this time. He'd let Alice onto the playing field and let her have a few minutes to worry about escaping. Then he'd finish her off with a surprise strike and start looking for his next victim.

The dramatic ringing of a loud gong startled Alice awake. She sat up and looked around, instantly in a state of high alert.

Hayward's voice blasted out of the loudspeaker like an announcer at a boxing match. "Time for the game to begin. You will go upstairs and take the door to the outside that you will find open. Step out and close the door behind you. I will give you twenty minutes to get as far away as you can."

She got up, did some stretches, and went to the bathroom. After using the facilities, she splashed water on her face and took a drink.

Although she wanted to reach into her pocket to feel the matches, she kept her hands at her sides as she walked down the hall and up the steps. The whole scene had feeling of unreality, like she was an actor in a play. But this scene was all too immediate.

"Keep your head, and keep your nerve," she told herself, knowing her only chance was to stay cool. Had the other women thought they could escape? Had they been paralyzed by fear and given up too easily? She certainly wasn't going to do that. If the bastard was going to finish her off, she wouldn't make it easy for him.

When she reached the top of the stairs, she saw the open door and stepped out. Instead of closing the door completely, she pulled it almost shut. Turning, she drew in a deep breath as she got her first taste of the outside since she'd arrived here. The sky was dark, but the moon was close to full, brightening the scene. The air was just a little chilly, and she was glad her shirt had long sleeves. Although it felt safer to linger in the doorway, she stepped away from the building, heading across a stretch of lawn. The grass felt dry and brittle under her feet, and she had the feeling that the rest of the summer had been dry.

The trees looked like they were beginning to turn. The idea of climbing one crossed her mind, but then she'd be trapped. Instead she headed to the other side of several old boxwoods and pressed backward into the small-leafed branches, enveloped by the bush's pungent aroma. When she had partially concealed herself, she reached into her pocket and pulled out the match-book. Flipping open the cover, she found that only about half the matches were still in the pack. Well, that was better than nothing.

Hayward had told her he'd give her twenty minutes to get away, which made her think that sticking around the house was a better idea.

Listening hard, she tried to detect any evidence of the man moving around the grounds, but she heard nothing.

Jonah, are you here Jonah? she called out.

At first there was no answer, and she repeated his name, hoping against hope that he was nearby.

Then the sound of someone calling *her* name made her almost cry out before she clamped her lips shut. She thought Hayward was trying to get her to break cover.

Then she realized the word had not been vocalized. It was in her head.

Jonah? My God, is that you? She had almost given up hope of seeing him tonight, but now he was here—calling her, and relief flooded through her.

Yes, he answered.

Where were you?

I had a little problem, but I'm here. Thank God I heard you calling. That got me over the hump.

What happened?

He hesitated for a moment. *I'll tell you later.*

What? she pressed.

It's a long story.

Something about the way he said it made her nerve endings tingle.

Focus on me, he said.

She did as he asked, and all at once he was standing almost beside her, his ghostly form shimmering in the moonlight. Like her, he seemed to be dressed in black. She reached for him, closing her eyes as she felt him move in close. He wrapped his arms around her, pulling her against his body.

I thought you weren't coming, she admitted.

I wasn't sure I could get here. But it looks like I made it. For a long moment, she clung to him, wishing he could hide her from Hayward. But she knew that was only a fantasy.

We have to get busy, he said before he eased away.

What are we going to do?

You stay here, he said. *I'm going to see if I can locate the bastard.*

Wait! I have matches. I stole them from his desk.

He drew in a quick breath. *The fire.*

What?

Stay here while I look for him.

She pressed farther into the bushes, watching Jonah stride away. Was she really going to make it out of here alive? Maybe with Jonah's help.

Her heart pounded as she waited in the moonlight. Finally she saw Jonah coming back.

He's in front, but he's coming this way.

What should I do?

I'm going to try the ghost trick again.

Jonah watched the bastard with the gun walk confidently around the side of the house. He seemed to be sure of Alice's location.

Shit. Jonah didn't know what kind of tracking equipment was available in the fifties, but this guy must have something. He'd told Alice he was giving her a chance to get away, but on the face of it, that must be a lie. If she escaped, she could turn him in, and he had to avoid that at all costs.

Jonah could hear something ticking as the man walked. The beeps got louder as he got closer to Alice. Christ, she must be wearing some kind of transmitter, and Hayward was following the sound. It was primitive by twenty-first century standards, but it was good enough to lead the killer to his victim.

He ran back to Alice. *Take off your shirt and pants. And your shoes, too.*

What?

He must have planted a transmitter in your clothes.

A what?

Something that will lead him to you. Take off your clothes and leave them on the ground. Then get away from them.

She stared at him, wide eyed.

Do it. I'll try to slow him down.

He ran back toward the killer, praying that Alice would do what he asked.

Alice stared after Jonah. She didn't really understand what he was talking about—but it made sense. There was a whole big estate where she could hide, and how would Hayward know in which direction she'd gone unless he had some way of keeping track of her? And hadn't he been very specific about what he wanted her to wear for this hunt? With her lower lip firmly between her teeth, she pulled off her shirt and threw it on the ground, to the right of where she was standing. Then she unzipped her pants and threw them on top of the shirt.

Her shoes followed. She had a heart-stopping moment when she realized the matches were still in the pants. Dashing out of the bush, she grabbed the pants and reached in the pocket.

They were gone!

No, wrong pocket.

Quickly she fumbled on the other side and found them.

Wearing only her bra and panties and feeling horribly vulnerable, she darted away from the clothing and into another clump of shrubbery, where she burrowed in as far as possible, thinking that with the dark clothing gone, she was going to stand out like a marble statue in the moonlight.

Faintly, she heard a clicking sound. It grew stronger as the man came around the corner. He stopped short, then turned to the place where she had discarded her clothing.

"Got ya," he shouted as he charged forward, then stopped a few yards from the bush where she'd been hiding.

"Son of a bitch," he shouted when he saw the garments lying on the ground. Then he bellowed her name. "Alice, you cunt, what the hell do you think you're doing?"

Jonah came up behind him and kicked him in the ass. He screamed and whirled around, pulling the trigger of the rifle he was holding. When it discharged, she silently screamed.

Jonah.

I'm fine.

Hayward turned in her direction again, and she cringed back into the bushes. For a terrible moment, she thought he had found her. Then he walked past her, heading for the formal garden. Jonah followed him, leaping in front of the man and waving his arms like he was desperately trying to stop a speeding car from plowing over a cliff. When Hayward ignored him, Jonah punched him in the face. The man howled, but he obviously couldn't see what had hit him. What did it even feel like? And would the killer keep heading for the garden?

When they were out of sight, she debated what to do—head for the hills or head back for the house? Either option was risky, but she liked going back the way she'd come.

She ran to the mansion and reached the door where she'd exited into the yard.

It was now shut tight.

Damn. She moved around the house looking for a way in, but all the windows were closed. When she tried some, she found they were locked.

Glancing over her shoulder, she couldn't see Hayward.

Are you still with him, she called to Jonah in her mind

Yes.

Where?

In the formal garden.

She headed to the other side of the house, looking up at the second story. When she spotted a window that was open about a foot, she looked for a way to get up and saw the drain pipe at the corner of the house.

There was no way the old Alice could have climbed it. But Hayward had made her work hard to get in shape. She reached as high as she could, grasped the pipe, and pulled herself up.

The metal held her weight. With the matchbook clamped between her teeth, she started moving upward, pulling with her strong arms and bracing with her feet. The metal dug into her bare soles, but she kept going.

Stopping at the window level, she swung one arm outward, grasped the edge of the open lower sash and pushed.

At first it wouldn't move. Then she put more force into the upward motion, and the sash opened a few more inches, enough for her to wiggle through.

When she climbed down to the floor, she saw she was in a bedroom. Hayward's bedroom, she figured, since there were coins and a wallet on the dresser.

She crossed to the closet, threw it open and saw shirts and suits hanging on a rack. Touching the man's clothes made her feel sick, but she snatched out a blue shirt and put it on, rolling up the sleeves as she turned to the bed.

Throwing back the spread, she took the matchbook from between her teeth, and struck a match. The first one she tried didn't catch. Tearing off another, she pressed more firmly. It caught, and she held it against the top sheet.

It immediately flared up, giving her a profound sense of satisfaction.

A pile of newspapers was on the bedside table, and she crumpled up several sheets, holding them in the flames until they caught, then tossed them around, one onto the rug and one onto the drapes.

As the flames leaped up, she exited the room and headed down the hall toward the stairs.

Alice. Her name rang in her head. *Alice, he's coming back. Where are you?*

In the house. I got upstairs. I've set his bedroom on fire.

Oh Christ. Get out of there.

Which way is he coming?

Toward where you dropped the clothes.

The bedroom behind her was blazing now, with smoke billowing out the door and down the hall, making her cough. She bent over, running down the stairs to a formal entrance which she had never seen before.

Jesus. Jonah's exclamation rang in her head. *He's seen the fire. He's running toward the front door Get out of there.*

She tried to comply, but smoke was pouring down the stairs now, making her dizzy. She dashed toward the back of the house and found the library where she and Hayward had talked earlier.

Picking up a paperweight from the desk, she smashed it into one of the windowpanes. When the glass broke, she ran to the opening, gulping in the fresh air as she fumbled to unlock the sash.

She had just gotten it up when Hayward came charging into the room, his eyes as blazing as the fire on the upper floor.

"You bitch," he screamed, raising the rifle.

She snatched a large book from the desk and threw it with all her might, hitting him in the head. He staggered back, but raised the gun again, one eye closed as he tried to focus on her.

Jonah was right behind him. In that instant, as he charged through the door, she saw him go from ghost to a solid figure.

She had no time to marvel at the change. Everything was happening too fast.

Hearing the running feet behind him, Hayward whirled.

"Christ! I see you," he shouted.

"Then stop picking on girls and fight like a man."

Hayward bent low and leaped toward him, knocking Jonah off his feet, and the two men rolled on the floor. When a gun went off, she gasped, but it looked like neither one of them had been hit.

A crackling sound made her look up, and she saw flames licking at the ceiling.

"Get out," Jonah shouted.

"Not without you."

The killer was on top of Jonah. She dashed to the fireplace, picked up the poker and brought it down on Hayward's head. He went still, and Jonah pitched him away, then struggled to his feet.

She was already yanking at the drapes, tearing them down and using the heavy fabric to pull away the broken glass at the window.

Jonah helped. When they had cleared away the shards, he shouted, "Go."

She hoisted herself up and clambered out, landing in a

flower bed. Jonah was seconds behind her. Grabbing her arm, he pulled her away from the house. They were twenty yards away when she turned to see that whole second floor was burning, with the flames creeping downward.

"Come on," Jonah cried, tugging at her arm. He was still a solid form, and she let him guide her away into the gardens.

She wanted to stop, but he made her keep moving, out of the landscaped area, across a field and into a small woods.

"Where are we going?" she gasped out.

"Away from this damn place."

At the edge of the woods, Jonah stopped and turned. The whole house seemed to be on fire now, and he could hear sirens in the distance.

Looking at Alice, he saw she was still dazed.

"Sweetheart, focus on me."

She blinked. "What?"

"We have to get away from here."

"Yes, I know," she answered, although she couldn't know what he meant.

He led her into the woods, then stopped. "Lord, I wasn't sure ..."

"But we're safe."

"Not quite yet. Come here." She came into his arms, and he folded her close, feeling her lean into him. "I have to take you back where I came from," he murmured as he stroked her back and shoulders.

"Can't we just run?"

"It's complicated. I came from farther away than you know." He swallowed hard. "To get there with me, you have to join your consciousness to mine."

"How?"

"Start by opening to me, like when we talk in our minds. Close your eyes. Make yourself part of me."

"I don't understand."

"You will. But you have to trust me. You have to be part of me," he repeated. "Like we talked in our heads. Only closer, deeper."

Trust me, he silently begged now.

I do. As she said it, he felt her opening herself to him in a way that would have seemed impossible a few days ago. Now it wasn't just words that bonded them together. He could read her emotions. He knew she was feeling his relief that he'd gotten her out of there and his joy in holding her. As she closed her eyes and leaned into him, he felt her coping with a jumble of his thoughts and her own. But he knew she could tell how important this was to him.

Her hands clamped onto his shoulders as the psychic lines between the two of them blurred.

He felt a dart of fear inside her. "What's happening?"

"I'm trying to bring you home with me. Relax. Don't fight me," he added, hearing a note of desperation in his own voice as he squeezed his eyes tightly closed and prayed that this would work.

"Trust me," he said again.

"I do," she answered, and he knew it was true. He clasped her more tightly, praying that he could take both of them back to his own time.

He felt a strong wind buffeting them, as though the gap in their times was holding her back.

"Come on, come on," he muttered, focusing on returning— with Alice.

A thunderclap shook them, and he heard her cry out.

His eyes flew open, and he looked toward the burning house. In the darkness, he could see nothing.

"I think we made it."

Opening her eyes, she stared at him, then reached up a hand to touch his lips, his brows, his cheeks.

"We're here together," he murmured, still taking it in, because until this moment, he hadn't known it was possible.

"What happened?"

"It's a long story," he answered thinking this was hard enough for him to comprehend, and that he had to ease her into this new reality.

But first, he couldn't stop himself from pulling her into his arms.

"You're free."

"Thanks to you."

She turned her face up to him, and it was the most natural thing in the world to lower his mouth to hers. They clung together, kissing and touching, the reality of her escape sinking in. As he held her and stroked her, he wanted her more than he had ever wanted a woman in his life. But he knew this place wasn't as safe as it seemed.

He tore his mouth away from hers and said. "We need to leave."

"Right now?"

"Yes. Come on."

He led her around some bushes, and she stopped short.

"That's my car," she gasped out. "Where did it come from?"

CHAPTER FOURTEEN

It was his turn to feel a jolt of shock. "Your car?"

"Yes. How did it get here?"

"I bought it—and drove it here."

"Bought it from whom?"

Jonah felt a shiver along his nerve endings. He had worried about this moment, but he'd thought he had more control over the revelation. "There's a lot I have to tell you. But uh . . . when did you buy the car?"

"I got it used a few months ago. I needed transportation, and it was what I could afford. I had driven it to the camp. I thought it was still in Western Maryland."

"Look back at the house," he murmured.

"The house? We were talking about the car."

"Uh huh."

She turned and looked across the fields, leaning forward.

"Where's the fire? I can't see it."

"We left it."

She looked confused.

"I need to tell you where we are and why you can't see the fire."

"Why not?"

"Because it was put out a long time ago."

"I don't understand. What do you mean?"

"Let's sit down."

"Is this going to be something very bad?"

"Yes—and no."

He escorted her to the passenger door, and she climbed into the front seat. He went around and slid behind the wheel, then turned to her.

"When I was trying to find you, I was having trouble figuring out where you were. Remember I asked you questions about what happened to you? I asked if Alice Davenport was your real name."

"I remember."

"That was because I couldn't find anything about an Alice Davenport dying in an accident in Western Maryland."

"Why not? That's what he told me he cooked up. Was he lying about that?"

Instead of answering, he went on. "I restore old cars. I was working on this car—your car—when I heard your voice over the radio."

"It's not old. Well some people would say it was, but I thought it was a good deal for the money."

Before he could untangle that for her, his cell phone rang. He pulled the instrument from his pocket and swiped his finger across the bottom of the screen.

"We're all waiting to find out what happened. Did you get her out of there?" Grant asked.

"Yes. Alice is here with me. She's fine."

"Where are you?"

"Back at the car," he answered, assuming Grant would know he was back in the twenty-first century if he'd answered the phone.

"It's her car. She bought it used in '61."

"That explains it."

"Yeah." He added, "I can't talk now. We'll be there soon."

"Understood." When he clicked off, he saw Alice watching him.

"Is that some kind of walkie-talkie?" she asked.

"Something like that."

"You said I bought the car in '61. That's this year, right?"

He felt his heart turn over. This was it. "No."

"Then what?"

He swallowed hard. "You know I'm telepathic. That's how I found you."

"Yes."

"When your voice came over the car radio, you were reaching across a lot of miles to find me. But it wasn't just miles. It was years, too."

She kept her gaze on him. "What do you mean?"

"You were in 1961. I wasn't."

She shook her head, grappling with that. "What year is it, then?"

When he told her the date in the twenty-first century she gasped. "No."

"I'm sorry."

She looked shell-shocked. "How?"

"I don't know. But it happened, and I was able to come back and find you. I didn't know what was really going on until yesterday. When we lost contact, I was following Hayward upstairs and into the kitchen and library. I found a calendar on the wall. I couldn't get close enough to read the date, but I saw it was from the Carvertown Business Association—so I knew what town you were in. And I saw a very distinctive rock in the river. My friend Grant Bradley and I rushed over here in a helicopter, and the house was burned up.

I thought I was too late. Then Grant pointed out it was an old fire."

"Oh my God. You mean from when I burned it?"

"Yeah."

As she started to shake, he pulled her close. He knew it was a lot to take in. He'd been just as shocked that morning when he'd realized what had happened.

"It's going to be okay."

"How?"

"We'll figure it out."

He felt her struggling for calm.

Raising her head, she searched his face. "And we can stay together?" she asked in a shaky voice.

"That's what you want?" He felt like he was in suspended animation. It was what he wanted, with all his heart.

"Yes."

Still, he had to say, "You don't know me well enough to make that decision."

"I think I do."

"I think we need more time. And I'm hoping you can stay here with me. But this place is going to be very strange for you."

He looked at the blue shirt she was wearing. "Maybe you want to put on some other clothes."

"What am I going to wear?"

"I told you I'm with a security company. Decorah Security. I keep spare clothes in the car for when I need to be away from home. They won't fit any better than what you're wearing."

"But they won't be his."

"Right."

He brought her a tee shirt, a light jacket and sweatpants. "I'm sorry I can't do anything about shoes. But a pair of thick socks will help."

She climbed out, and he turned away while she pulled off the blue shirt and dressed.

"Okay."

When he turned back, he said, "Very cute."

"But you're right, they're too big."

"Part of the cuteness."

Suddenly he could see she was a little shy. It made him realize that she'd lived in an era before women's lib and the sexual revolution. That was going to make her values a little different from his.

He dragged in a breath and let it out. "A lot will be familiar. Like those clothes. But in some ways you're like Sleeping Beauty—without the sleep."

"Like how?"

"We have all kinds of things you never imagined. Personal computers." He laughed. "I think you didn't have any computers at all."

"Maybe big companies did. But I'm not sure what they are."

"Machines that process information very fast. They used to take up a whole room. Now they fit into something like this." He held up his cell phone. "It's got a computer in it. A lot of things do. Cars. TV's. Home security systems." He laughed. "Even sewing machines."

She nodded slowly. "What's going to surprise me most?"

"Hum. Well, you can heat up food in a few minutes in a microwave. A lot of people order their clothes and anything else they need online and have it delivered."

"Online?"

"Using high speed communications. Better than the Sears Catalogue—which is out of business. There are a lot of diseases that can be cured now." He laughed. "From the sublime to the ridiculous, Elvis got to be a big star, but he got fat and died."

"No!"

"A lot of people think he's really alive and hiding some-where. It's a big folk legend. His home in Nashville is a shrine." He thought for a moment. "And in other music news, Bob Dylan got the Nobel Prize for Literature."

"You're kidding."

"Cross my heart and hope to die."

There were a lot of other more shocking developments he could tell her about—like terrorism, police brutality, "group mentality" generated by social media, fake news, and climate change.

But he figured it was better not to jump into that kind of stuff.

Scrambling for something else she'd like to hear, he said, "They still have Milky Ways, Mounds, and Snickers bars."

She tipped her head to the side. "Those are your candy bars of choice?"

"Yeah." Switching back to business, he said, "I'd like to take you to Decorah Security headquarters. You can stay there for a few days while you decide what you want to do."

Her features registered panic. "I'd rather stay with you."

"My place isn't exactly plush. It's an apartment over an old garage."

"That's fine."

"I hope so," he answered. Did she want to stay with him because he was the only person she knew here? Or did she want to be with him as much as he wanted her?

"I told Grant we'd be starting back."

She nodded, and he turned the key in the ignition.

His nerves were jumping as he made the two-hour drive back to Beltsville. On the way, he told Alice more about life in the twenty-first century.

Trying to think of big and little differences, he said, "They figured out cigarettes are bad for you. Hardly anyone smokes them. Some people switched to electronic cigarettes."

Her brow wrinkled. "What are they?"

"They deliver nicotine vapor. That's the active ingredient in tobacco."

"Okay."

"There are lots of fast-food restaurants—also not good for you."

"Fast food? What is it and why is it bad?"

"It's stuff you can get in a few minutes. Like McDonald's. They had that in the fifties and sixties, right?"

"Yes."

"Well, there are tons more. Other hamburger chains plus pizza, Mexican, even fish. But their meals are loaded with calories. The U.S. population is getting heavier."

How had he gotten off onto talking about fast food? He felt like he was babbling, but he couldn't settle down, and he kept trying to add more details about modern life.

"People dress more casually. And, I guess you could say society isn't as civil."

"What does that mean?"

"People are less polite. They curse more."

"Tell me something good."

"There's a big movement not to raise and kill animals for their fur. Instead, there are very good synthetic furs. You don't have to break your fingernails dialing a phone. They have push buttons. And you're not tied to a phone cord. You can take the receiver out of a charging station and walk around the house with it. And, oh yeah, a 'caller ID' will show you who's on the other end of the line before you answer."

"That sounds good."

"Well unless they don't want you to know who they are. Then it might say 'unknown.'"

Trying for more good news, he said, "We still have the old TV networks, but there are more than 300 channels."

She blinked. "How is that possible?"

"You get them by cable—or with a satellite dish."

"Which is?"

"An antenna that brings in wireless transmissions. Some channels have news all day. There's a golf channel. A weather channel. Home and garden. Disney. A couple of channels that are like big commercials all day—designed to sell you everything from jewelry and china to fashions and toys."

She shook her head, trying to take it in.

"And there's so many other outlets for news and information that newspapers and magazines are going out of business."

"Really?"

"Unfortunately."

"And you don't have to buy paper books. You read them on your phone or a tablet—which is a little bigger."

As they turned onto an access road leading to Decorah Security, Alice stared at a line of long low buildings made of what looked like artificial stone blocks.

"Your company has all this?"

"No, we're in an industrial park."

"A what?"

"There are lots of businesses in these buildings. Technology firms. Service companies. We have several of the adjoining units here because we want to be unobtrusive. And the rent's cheap."

They pulled up in front of an entrance door with only a small sign giving the firm's name.

When they got out, she whispered, "I'm nervous."

"Don't be. Everybody here is a friend."

Still, she reached for his hand as they headed down a short sidewalk.

In the reception area, an older man with salt and pepper hair stepped toward them. His eyes were glowing as he clasped Jonah on the shoulder.

"You did it."

"Yeah, I guess I did." Jonah's face broke into a broad grin.

Alice took in the exchange. She'd been so caught up in her own drama that she hadn't thought about the enormity of what Jonah had accomplished. He'd rescued her in another time—then brought her home with him. Probably nobody had ever done it before.

As she was coming to grips with that reality, the man turned to her. His keen eyes searched her face. "I'm glad you made it here."

His voice and his expression told her that he was thrilled that she'd arrived safe and sound.

"I'm Frank Decorah. We've all been anxious to meet you."

"I'm glad . . . to be here," she stammered.

"We'll try not to overwhelm you."

She nodded, seeing the other people in the room were hanging back. Two women and two men, none dressed the way she'd expect in a business office. All of them had on jeans and tee shirts or knit tops. The men looked like twins. And all of them seemed to be around Jonah's age. One of the guys shook Jonah's hand.

"Congratulations."

"Yeah, well I couldn't have done it if you hadn't given me a lot of pointers."

"But you're the one who did the heavy lifting."

Jonah nodded and turned to Alice. "This is Grant Bradley. He did something similar when his wife, Jen, was being held captive."

"But not across any years," Grant pointed out.

Jonah went on with the introductions—to Grant's twin brother Mack. And their wives, Jen and Rachel.

"How are you doing?" Mack's wife, Rachel, asked, and Alice sensed it wasn't a casual question.

"Okay," she answered. "Well, maybe stunned is a better way to put it."

"You'll settle in," Rachel said. She cleared her throat. "I'm a physician. Jonah has kept us informed about what was going on with you. Now that you're here, I'd like to give you a quick physical."

Alice nodded, looking at the small crowd again. "I'm so grateful to be here."

"It will take some adjustment," Frank Decorah said. "Modern life has its advantages—and downsides."

"Jonah was telling me some things."

"We're all here to help you."

Rachel put a hand on her arm. "We should do the exam—so I can clear you for normal activity."

CHAPTER FIFTEEN

In the Decorah infirmary, which looked a lot like a doctor's office, Alice sat on an exam table while Rachel—the doctor had said to call her Rachel—did a routine physical—listening to her heart and lungs, taking her blood pressure, testing her reflexes.

"All good," she said as she made notations on a screen, using something that looked like a flat typewriter keyboard.

"Is that a computer?"

"Yes. I guess you haven't seen one."

"Only Jonah's phone. He said that was a computer."

"Yes. This is a laptop. It's connected to a bigger data storage unit. I can make notes and call them up any time I want. And, of course, they take up less space than paper records."

Alice nodded. "So you work for Decorah Security?"

"Yes. I run the Decorah facility for patients who are in a coma."

"You do?"

"Yes. Their brains are all hooked up to a virtual reality."

"A what?"

"A place that's not real. It's all electronic—inside a big computer." She flapped her arm in frustration. "I'm no good at explaining the technical part. But it's a very special program that Decorah is running. Although the patients are unconscious, from their point of view, they're living in a very plush hotel."

"I don't understand."

Rachel laughed. "It's pretty unusual. Even for this day and age. One of the technicians can explain when we have more time. Right now I'm going to take some blood so we can check out things like your glucose level, your red and white cell counts, cholesterol and a few other things."

"What's cholesterol?"

"I guess the short answer is—fat in your blood."

"I haven't had much fat lately. He had me on a healthy diet," she said, not wanting to use the man's name.

Rachel picked up on that and said, "Jonah told Grant the guy was going to hunt you—like exotic game."

She shuddered. "Yes. He told me he'd killed five other women."

"And you escaped."

"I wouldn't have—without Jonah. He figured out that the guy put a tracker on me. He wasn't going to let me get away. He knew exactly where I was. He must have played the same game with the other women—letting them think they had a chance to escape."

"That's pretty horrible." Rachel cleared her throat. "I have to ask—did he abuse you?"

Alice gave the doctor a direct look. "If confining me in a cell, giving me tasteless food, and forcing me to exercise my head off is abuse, then yes. But if you mean—did he rape me? No. It seemed like keeping me under his control and planning the hunt was the way he got his pleasure out of the situation."

"And you came through it."

"I think I was resigned to staying alive as long as I could—before the end."

The doctor drew in a breath.

"Jonah saved me in another way. I had almost given up hope. But when he spoke to me mind to mind, it was like my whole world changed."

"Yes."

Suddenly she blurted the worry that had been clawing at her. "There are so many things here I don't understand."

'You're smart. You will.'

"But do you think I can fit in—and Jonah and I could make a relationship work?"

"I hope so. Because I know he cares about you. When he lost the communication with you, he got frantic."

"Me too." She swallowed hard. "Now that the emergency is over, I hope we're not too different to understand each other."

"We know you're going to have to get your bearings. And you're welcome to stay in our guest suite for a while."

She shook her head. "I appreciate the offer, but I'm going home with Jonah."

"Okay."

"You don't approve?" she asked quickly.

"It's your decision—and his."

"He agreed."

The doctor nodded and cleared her throat. "It's a good idea for you to use birth control if you make love with him."

Shocked by the bluntness, Alice felt herself flush. "I don't know much about it."

"Right, in your era a girl your age probably wouldn't."

"So you're saying he'll find me . . . naive?"

"No, I think he'll like it that he's the man who made you want to take the next step."

She nodded, wondering if it really was true.

"There are birth control methods for women, but they all require a prescription. Ask him to use a condom," Rachel said.

She flushed again. "Uh . ."

"They had them back then, right?"

"Yes, but I never needed to use one."

"It's part of being responsible." The doctor turned away, opened a drawer and handed Alice a couple of packets. "Here. You can put them in your pocket. Her voice turned brisk. "And let's ditch those oversize guy clothes for something that fits. We keep a lot of things on hand here in case a client needs something."

Alice was glad about the change of subject. It felt strange discussing something as private as sex with a woman she'd just met. But the woman was a doctor, Alice reminded herself. She could even ask her more questions, if she weren't too embarrassed to do it.

Rachel led her down the hall to a room with closets on three sides and drawers on the other. Together they found a pair of stylish jeans, a pretty mint green knit top and running shoes. Rachel also got out a suitcase and put in extra underwear, some tee shirts, and a couple more outfits.

"And what about some makeup?" Rachel asked.

They moved to another section of the room where Alice found products she recognized. She put on lipstick, a little blusher, and some subtle eye shadow.

"Nice," Rachel approved as she added Alice's choices to the suitcase.

"Thanks. But you know, I'm overwhelmed by all this."

"Frank Decorah is very generous with clients."

"Am I a client?"

"Yes."

"But I can't pay him. At least not yet."

"Don't worry about that. He had funds set up for people in need."

"Charity cases?"

"I wouldn't put it that way. In the first place, your making it here has given Decorah invaluable information."

As they stepped into the hall, Alice could see the men deep in conversation. They stopped talking and glanced up.

She caught the appreciative look in Jonah's eye as he took in her appearance.

She smiled at him, then turned to Frank, who was evaluating her on a more basic level—with a mixture of concern and speculation.

"Are you okay?" he asked.

"I'm still marveling at my miraculous escape."

"I can imagine."

The way he said it sent a little shiver over her skin, and she had the feeling he had a better idea of her feelings than the others. Had he been through something similar?

She'd have to ask Jonah later.

"It would help if you could write a report of your impressions of contacting Jonah and everything that happened after that. The paranormal experience—from your point of view."

"Of course."

"I should get you home," Jonah said, "You probably want to get some rest."

"Right." She hoped he had just said that for the benefit of the others. Resting wasn't at the top of her current list.

They got back into the Chevy, and he drove through the darkness, to an area that still looked fairly rural. Their destination was a country garage.

"Frank found this place for me. He got the owner to sell for practically nothing. I put in a lot of sweat equity turning the wasted space upstairs into an apartment."

In the service bays they passed several vehicles that she might have seen on the street. He got her suitcase from the backseat and carried it up a flight of stairs. At the door to his apartment, he hesitated. "It's nothing fancy."

"I don't need fancy."

"I should have straightened up."

"Please, don't worry about it."

The comments told her he was nervous, too.

He unlocked the door and led her into a large space that was part living room and part kitchen.

As he set down her suitcase, she looked around. The kitchen was arranged in an L-shape with a refrigerator, stove and sink along the back wall. A perpendicular counter came out at an angle. In the middle of the L was a wooden table and four chairs.

Across the room were a worn couch and an easy chair. An empty glass sat on an end table and a pair of shoes and socks were on the floor. Really, not much was out of order. Her gaze went to a large flat screen hanging on the wall across from the couch.

"What's that?"

"My TV. They got a lot more streamlined. You don't need that bulky cathode ray tube anymore."

He picked up something about the size of a small, flat flashlight, pointed it at the TV, and clicked a button. She blinked as the screen flashed to life. It was in bright colors, like a Technicolor movie. Two men were discussing a baseball game.

"Like I said, we have hundreds of channels." He flicked another button. "And you don't have to get up to change."

Bits and pieces of other scenes flashed by. What looked like a newscast. A cartoon. A drama. Then a scene of a man and a woman in a tight clinch. They were kissing hotly, and the man reached for the zipper at the back of her dress.

Jonah clicked it off. "Sorry about that."

"Don't be. I think it's a suggestion."

"Of what?"

"What we both want to do."

"Alice. . . ."

Sensing that he wasn't going to push her into anything, she reached for him and pulled him close.

He said her name again, his voice full of longing.

"Don't step away from me because you think it's the right thing to do," she whispered.

"It is. You've been through a horrible ordeal. You just got here. I could be taking advantage of you."

"Of course not. I want to be as close to you as I can get."

Cupping the back of his hair, she brought his head down. He moved his lips against hers, and she opened for him, reveling in the intimate contact. Accepting the invitation, his tongue played with the line of her teeth and the sensitive tissue just beyond her lips.

That simple contact sent currents of heat coursing through her. And when he lifted his head, they were both breathing hard.

His hands stroked up and down her back. "Have you . . . made love before?" he asked.

"Are you asking because I seem . . ." she fumbled for a phrase and came up with, "Wet behind the ears?"

"No. I'm making assumptions because of . . . when you come from. You were probably taught—good girls don't."

Rachel had made the same assumptions. Alice dragged in a breath and let it out. "You're right. My parents were pretty strict with us. I haven't gone all the way before. But I want to—with you."

"Why?"

"You saved my life."

"And you want to thank me."

"No, I want to finish what we started. She stopped talking

and said the last part silently. *I mean, we were so close. In each other's minds. It was unique. And wonderful. And being in your arms is another kind of wonderful.*

She felt him shudder. *On Lord, Alice.*

I think it's going to work out, she said, putting as much conviction as she could muster into the assertion.

When she lifted her face again, he brought his lips back to hers for a kiss that was both hungry and gentle.

They stood kissing and swaying in the middle of the room, and she felt as if the apartment was whirling around her.

"You're making my head spin," she murmured, speaking aloud against his lips.

"Mine too."

"Can we lie down?"

"You mean sit down?"

"I think your bed is probably more comfortable than your couch—for anything major."

He dragged in a breath and let it out before leading her through a door to a bedroom that was about the same size as the living room. When he switched on a bedside lamp, she saw that his bed was wide, with a spread carelessly pulled up. A chair in one corner was piled with clothes he'd worn.

"Sorry it's not neater."

"It's fine."

Not sure exactly what to do next, she sat down on the edge of the mattress and kicked off her shoes. Then she decided to pull off her jeans. She was about to toss them on the floor when she remembered they had something she needed.

"Rachel told me to use a condom," she said as she fumbled in the right front pocket and pulled out the packets.

He made a low sound. "You talked about this?"

"Not much. But I told her I wanted to be with you, and she said we should be responsible."

She handed him the packets, which he put on the night table. She gave them a quick look before pulling off the jeans and slipping under the covers, leaving space beside her. He turned the light down to a lower setting, then pulled his tee shirt over his head. Although he kicked off his shoes, he kept his jeans on as he slipped under the covers beside her.

"I've got a shirt and you've got pants," she said, then felt like it was a dumb comment.

"Not for long." He folded her into his arms, and she snuggled against his broad chest.

He rolled to his side, kissing her again, playing with her mouth as his hands began to stroke her back, her ribs, the curve of her hip. His touch was light, but it felt like his fingers were trailing fire down her sensitized skin.

She didn't want to be a passive lover. She flattened her hand against his chest, feeling his heart beating and loving the texture of his masculine skin and the hair spreading out in a wide pattern. When her hand brushed his nipple, he caught his breath.

"Is that okay?"

"Oh yeah. I can show you." Sweeping the covers aside, he helped her to a sitting position, then eased the knit shirt over her head. As he lay her back down, he dipped his finger into the top edge of her bra, playing with her breasts, stroking downward. Her nipples tightened, and when he finally touched one, she felt a jolt of sensation. Bending over, he pressed his lips against the other peak, using his mouth on her through the thin fabric of her bra.

"Oh!"

Reaching behind her, she unfastened the hooks, then pulled the bra away.

As he stared down at her, she held her breath. Would he think her breasts were too small?

"You're so pretty."

"I want to be. For you."

"You're perfect. Just right for my hands."

He cupped both breasts, stroking sensually, then drew circles around her nipples, making them rise to rigid nubs, as the circles drew inward. And when he finally brushed his fingers against their sides, she couldn't hold back an exclamation.

"That's so good."

"God, yes. I love the way you respond to me."

"How?"

He grinned. "With heat."

"Yes, heat." As he gathered her close, kissing and caressing her, she felt her whole body flame. She had made out with guys, but they had never made her feel like this. Nobody had been this experienced—or as focused on giving her pleasure.

He watched her face as one of his hands slid down her body, into her panties, winnowing through the triangle of hair at the juncture of her legs before slipping into the folds of her sex. They were swollen and slick and exquisitely sensitive.

He stroked down to her vagina, dipping inside as he had before, then up to her clitoris, and she raised her hips into the caress.

"I touched you like this when I was a ghost. I wanted to give you as much pleasure as I could. "

"You did."

"Had you done that before?"

"No."

"But you let me."

"You made me feel alive for the first time in months."

When she reached to press her hand against the bulge at the front of his jeans, he drew in a quick breath.

Feeling bold, she undid his belt buckle and the button at the waistband before lowering the zipper and thrusting her hand into his shorts so that she was touching him intimately.

He felt full and hot and very large.

"That's going to fit inside me?" she heard herself ask.

"Yes, but we don't have to do everything tonight."

"I want to do everything. It's my reward for surviving."

He seemed to stop breathing as he watched her pull down her panties and toss them onto the floor.

He did the same with his jeans and shorts. Before she could get a good look at him, he pulled her into his arms, his hot flesh molding to hers.

She pressed against his penis, loving the way it teased her throbbing center.

He kept her in a tight embrace, clasping her bottom, stroking her back.

She couldn't stop herself from moving against him, rocking against his hard shaft.

"I think it's time."

He rolled away, and she saw him open one of the packets she had put on the night table.

When he came back to her, she tensed, thinking he was going to thrust himself inside her right away. Instead, he played with her breasts again, then slid himself against her the way he had done with his hand, giving her long, sensual strokes.

She threw back her head, absorbing the sensations, helpless to do anything but quicken to the exquisite friction.

She felt herself driving for climax, knowing she was close. She needed only a few more strokes before she tumbled over the edge and flew off into the clouds. And as her orgasm began to fade, she felt him lift her hips and change the angle as he drove into her.

There was a moment of pain, but only a moment. Then he

was moving urgently inside her, pushing for his own satisfaction, his hips rising and falling.

He cried out, breathing hard, shuddering as he came down on top of her.

She kissed his cheek, stroked her hands over his sweat-slick back.

When he rolled to his side, he took her with him.

She snuggled against his chest, marveling at how well he had planned that. He had given her the ultimate pleasure before ever taking his own.

Thank you, she said.

Are you okay?

Yes, that was wonderful. And there's no way to lie mind to mind.

"I didn't want to hurt you," he said, switching to speech again, and she smiled at the way they could change the way they talked to each other.

"Only a little. You did it just right"

He fumbled with the condom, crumpled it into a tissue and threw it on the floor before taking her back into his arms.

She cuddled against him and whispered, "I thought I was going to die in that hunt, and you charged in on a white horse. No a '55 Chevy."

"Because you called out to me."

"Without much hope."

"That makes it even more remarkable."

"More like desperate."

CHAPTER SIXTEEN

Alice stayed in Jonah's arms, drifting on a tide of contentment—and wonder, still trying to believe this was all real—and that everything could have changed so completely.

Finally he stirred, "I hate to break the spell, but did you eat today?"

The question made her think again how everything was different. "I was too nervous to eat much."

"Me too. I didn't know if I could get back there again once I realized I had to travel through time, and I didn't know what I could do to help when I got there."

"You helped plenty. Just telling me about the tracker saved my life."

"Thank God. And now let's get practical. What do you want to eat?"

"What are my choices?"

"I make a pretty good omelet. Or I have pizza in the freezer."

"I'd love the omelet, if it's not too much trouble."

"No, that's good. Do ham, onion, green pepper and cheese work for you?"

"Yes."

"I'll give you some privacy."

"Thanks."

She waited while he dressed. When he'd left the room, she grabbed her clothes and ducked into the bathroom.

Turning toward the sink, she inspected her face in the mirror. Her cheeks were leaner than she remembered. But her eyes were bright, and she looked like a very satisfied woman.

She'd said making love was her reward for surviving. But survival was still astonishing, after all she had been through.

She cleaned up a little, dressed, and left the bedroom. In the kitchen, Jonah was chopping onions on a cutting board made of some material she'd never seen before.

"What can I do?"

"Chop the pepper and the ham."

He pulled out a small skillet, then put it back and got out a larger one. "Easier to make a big omelet and cut it in half."

"Right."

The ham was sliced in a package, and she cut some of the slices into smaller pieces, then watched him sauté the ingredients in olive oil. Her mom would have used butter, but the oil sounded more interesting.

Every small thing was mind-blowing because fixing a meal was so normal, when her whole life had been a nightmare for months. While the onion, pepper and ham were cooking, he cracked six eggs into a bowl and scrambled them.

The cheese was already shredded and in a plastic package which he opened by tearing the top, then sealing it again with a hidden strip. She watched everything, determined to learn how this place worked.

Instead of flipping the big omelet, he put the cheese on top when the eggs were almost done, then put on a lid to finish the cooking.

In no time they were sitting across from each other at the wooden table.

"You said nobody smokes. But I saw beer in your refrigerator."

"You want some?"

"No, but you go ahead. Do you have any tea?"

"I think I can find herbal tea. Some of the Decorah guys drink it."

"Why?"

"Long story. I'll tell you when you know them better."

"Grant and Mack?"

"No, some of the other agents."

When he got up, she said, "I didn't mean for you to go to any trouble."

"No trouble." He found a box of assorted herbal tea bags in a cabinet and let her choose.

She picked cranberry. He put the tea bag in a mug and added water. Then he put it in a rectangular appliance hanging over the stove. A minute later, he took out a steaming mug.

"That's the microwave thing?"

"Yes. And you have to be careful because the container you put in comes out hot. Also, food heats according to how much there is. A little takes a short time. Something larger takes longer. It's better for warming food than for actually cooking."

She listened carefully, taking in another lesson.

"I don't even know what you did for a living."

"I was a junior high school English teacher."

"It's called middle school now. That's still a career you can have—although you'll need to get used to doing grades and other stuff with a computer. And probably the breakdown in grammar skills will make you weep."

"But I have no teaching credentials here."

"Frank and I talked about that. Decorah Security will have to give you a new identity."

"How?"

"We find someone who died as a baby, and you pretend you're her."

"Is that legal?"

"No. But it works. You'll need a driver's license, a library card, a social security number. All kinds of stuff." He dragged in a breath and let it out. "It's going to be confusing, but no worse than an immigrant coming here from a third world country."

"Which is?"

"A country that's not modernized, and the standard of living is low. Newcomers have to learn all kinds of stuff."

"Okay," she answered, but she felt way out of her depth.

"I know it's all hard to take in."

"We can go back to bed, and you can make me forget about it. And then you can clue me in to more hard reality in the morning."

"Good idea." They both stood.

"I should help you do the dishes."

"I have a dishwasher."

"I know there were people who did back in my time. But we didn't have one on the farm." On the last word, her voice broke, and she felt her eyes fill with tears.

Rushing around the table, he reached for her, gathered her to him and sat down, lowering her into his lap.

As her body shook, he stroked her tenderly, pressing her face to his shoulder.

"I'm getting you all wet," she said between sobs.

"It's okay. Everything is going to be okay."

"I mentioned the farm, and it made me think about my family."

"I figured."

"It just struck me that I'm never going to see them again."
She gulped as she struggled for control of her emotions.

"Do you want me to take you back?"

"Could you?"

"I don't know."

She swallowed. "I think it was hard to get me here—judging
from the reaction of the people at Decorah."

"Yes."

She raised her face, dashing away the tears on her cheeks
with the side of her hand. "You said you might be able to take
me back. What if we could go back and stop Hayward?"

"What do you mean?"

"Find out when he started kidnapping women. Stop him
from doing it."

"I don't know. That sounds like a hard job."

She knew he was right, and she wasn't going to spoil this
first evening with him by pressing the issue.

CHAPTER SEVENTEEN

They cleaned up the kitchen together, then returned to the bedroom where they made love again. It was better than the first time because now Alice didn't need to be shy. And instead of waiting until the last second to enter her, Jonah did it much sooner, then tantalized her with long slow strokes until she was frantic to climax.

"Jonah. Please."

"You need to come?" he asked, his voice teasing.

"Is that what it's called?" she asked. Grasping his butt, she pulled him close and forced the issue.

She was limp with satisfaction, as she lay next to him, but couldn't help thinking about her idea—of stopping Hayward. Something about it felt dangerous. But she was too tired to figure out why.

In the morning, she woke with a start, expecting to find herself in her cell. Instead, she was with Jonah, and she breathed out a little sigh of relief as she moved closer to him.

"You okay?" he murmured.

"I guess this isn't all a dream," she whispered.

"Not at all." He reached for her hand and knitted his fingers with hers.

"It's real," she whispered.

"Oh, yeah." He rolled so he could sling a leg over hers and brush her hair back from her face.

She felt herself responding to the sexual invitation and had to say, "We ran out of condoms."

"There are plenty of other fun ways to come. Like what we did that first time." To illustrate, he slid his hand up her thigh.

When he had left her relaxed and satisfied, she asked, "And I can do that for you?"

"Uh huh."

"How?"

"You can wrap your hand around my cock."

"On the farm, that's a rooster."

"Not here." He folded her fingers around his shaft, showing her how to pump up and down.

"Another new word for my English teacher's dictionary?" she said as she learned what he liked. It felt intimate to do it, and she loved watching his face as his passion built, and his hips began to thrust.

Afterwards, she cuddled against him for long moments, then said, "Is it going to sound weird if I tell you I want to go for a run?"

He grinned. "Not after the way you've been spending your days. And I run almost every morning. How far do you want to go?"

"I don't know. I used a treadmill, but I couldn't tell the mileage."

"I'll take you on a route I like, and when you think you've done about half of your usual, we'll turn around."

He let her set the pace, running easily alongside. It turned out that the trip out and back was five miles.

"Wow!" she said. "Five miles. I didn't know I could go that far."

"And you're not even winded. You could have done more. You've got stamina."

They came in and showered together, which delayed their leaving for the office.

"And we stop at a drugstore on the way," she insisted.

He shook his head. "I'm afraid your picture of a drugstore is going to change radically."

They drove in the car he usually used, a Honda with all kinds of features she'd never seen before—like an ignition that didn't require a key, headrests and a warning that forced you to use a seat belt.

And he was right about the drugstore. It was as large as a supermarket in her day, and had aisle after aisle of health and personal care products she didn't recognize. Plus other shelves were full of things she might have expected to find in a five and dime. Expect there were no nickel and dime items. The prices made her jaw drop in shock.

"How can anyone afford this stuff?" she asked as they left with their purchase in a white plastic bag.

"Well, salaries are higher—although they haven't kept pace with the cost of living. A lot of middle-class jobs have gone overseas where labor is cheaper."

"You'll have to explain that to me."

"People in countries like Vietnam don't make as much as Americans, so the goods shipped from there are cheaper."

"Wait a minute. Vietnam? Wasn't that a Communist country—and we were sending troops there?"

"Not anymore."

"What about the Russians?"

"That's complicated."

"Are we still in a Cold War with them?"

"The short answer is "no." We can sit down and talk about geopolitics later."

When they arrived at the office, Frank was already there.

"I was hoping you'd come in," he said to Alice.

"Why?"

"I wanted to see how you're doing."

"And I wanted to talk to you about an idea I had."

"Then let's all get comfortable."

They retired to one of the staff lounges. Jonah and Alice sat together on the couch. Frank took one of the easy chairs opposite.

"You look like things are working out," he remarked as he noted their relaxed appearance.

Jonah grinned. Alice felt her face redden a little and wished she could stop reacting like a nervous virgin.

Because she was embarrassed about Frank's imagining their night together, she jumped right in, "I want to talk about stopping . . . Hayward."

His gaze sharpened. "Explain what you mean."

"What if we could find out when he took his first victim and . . . kill him first?"

"You're talking about murder?"

She raised her chin. "Technically, yes, I guess. But we'd wait until he was capturing the first woman. That would be proof of what he was going to do. Then it would be . . . legitimate to stop him, wouldn't it?"

"That sounds right, but we'd better nail some stuff down before you go any further."

The tone of Frank's voice put her on alert.

"What?" they both asked.

"When Jonah came to you at the estate, he was like a 'ghost.' He wasn't solid. He couldn't touch anything."

"But at the end, he got to be himself."

"Did he?" Frank asked.

"I haven't written up a report of last night yet—but yeah, I did it."

"What happened to change you?" Frank asked.

"It was when Hayward charged into the house to kill Alice. In that moment, I knew I had to stop him. And the only way I could do it was to turn into flesh and blood."

"You think you can do it again?" Frank asked. "When you're not in the middle of an emergency."

"I guess I'd have to find out."

"And take Alice with you?"

He hesitated. "That may not be necessary."

Frank looked like he might argue. Instead, he said, "Let's assume you can go as yourself—not a ghost—and show up to stop Hayward's taking the first victim."

Jonah nodded.

Frank turned to Alice. "You say there were five other women."

"That's what he told me."

"We'd have to figure out who they were."

"All of them or just the first one?" Alice asked.

"All," Frank answered. "Because we'd need to know how they fit into the timeline. What if it was someone important who could change history by not getting killed?"

Alice shook her head. "I came to you all excited about this. Now I see I didn't think it through."

"But it might be okay. We'd have to do a lot of research. And there's one more important point," Frank said. "You'd have a big decision."

"About what?"

"You told Jonah that Hayward made it look like you died in a rock fall."

"Yes."

"So as far as the world is concerned, you're supposed to be dead—under thousands of tons of rock."

"Yes."

"But if Hayward never captured you, you'd have kept on with your normal life."

She nodded, wondering where this was going.

"If you kept on with your life, you would not have met Jonah."

She felt her heart stop, then start up again in double time. Oh Lord, she'd been so anxious to save the murder victims that she hadn't considered a lot of important points. And this was the most critical. She swung toward the man beside her, knowing in that instant how much he meant to her. "I . . . have to meet him."

"Then we'd have to go back and make the fake accident happen," he said, his voice calm and reassuring.

"Oh God. What if it doesn't work?" Her head was spinning now.

"You'll be stuck in your old life," Frank said. "I think you won't even know Jonah existed. And of course, there'd be no chance of your meeting because he wasn't born until decades later."

The devastated look of strain on Jonah's face made her want to weep. Instead she threw herself into his arms, holding him with all her might.

But as she clung to him, she knew she had no alternative. The moment she'd thought of saving those women, the course had been set. If she didn't carry out her plan, she was as good as killing them.

CHAPTER EIGHTEEN

Alice had come to see Frank because she'd wanted to convince him they could thwart a serial killer. The Decorah chief had outlined some of the obstacles they'd have to face—before dealing the ultimate soul-crushing blow.

Her happiness was at stake. And not just hers. She could see from Jonah's face that the prospect of losing her was unthinkable.

Yet she could also see he was the kind of man who wasn't going to let five women die—if he could help it.

He gave her a dark look. "I don't know what chance we have of pulling it off, but this mission isn't as easy as my homing in on your voice over the radio."

She nodded, waiting for him to put up more obstacles.

"We don't even know who these women are yet. But when we find out, we'll have to go back to a specific day and time—and hope we have enough information to succeed."

She could feel her throat closing, but she managed to say, "Then we'll have to do a lot of research to figure out who they are and when they were taken."

Jonah said, "I guess our first step is to see the office IT

specialist, Teddy Granada. Don't be put off by him. He looks like he's been wearing the same clothes for weeks, but he knows his way around the Internet like a monkey in a banyan forest."

Alice turned to Frank. "Thank you for agreeing to try."

"I can agree, but it's only gonna happen if Jonah can pull it off."

She gave him an apologetic look. "I put a lot on you. In more ways than one."

"And what if I disappoint you?"

"I'll know that you tried your hardest."

He answered with a tight nod before taking her down the hall to a room full of computers and other equipment and introduced Teddy.

They grabbed chairs and got into the facts of the case.

"We're assuming the women all supposedly died in accidents, but really they were abducted and held by a serial killer before he forced them to participate in a game where he hunted and killed them."

Teddy made a low noise. "Nice guy."

"Our search should start with newspaper accounts of women who went missing and were never found," Jonah said. "And presumed dead."

"I guess it's possible he could have skipped the accident part with some of them—if he thought he could get away with it," Alice added.

"How many women?" Teddy asked.

"Five," Alice answered.

The IT specialist picked at a hangnail. "That's a lot of victims to locate from that long ago."

"I know. Sorry."

"Let me see what I can turn up."

After the session, Jonah said, "We don't have to work every minute."

"I guess that's right."

"Let's go out and have some fun."

She blinked. "Just like that?"

"Right. You're entitled."

She nodded, because anything would be fine with her, if she spent the time with Jonah.

He thought for a few moments. "You'd probably like the Baltimore Inner Harbor. It was a sleazy port area until it got redeveloped as a big tourist attraction. There are boats moored along the quay, an aquarium, shopping pavilions, restaurants. We can wander around and have some lunch."

They ate at a seafood restaurant on the waterfront, then spent the afternoon taking in the sights.

As they sat on a park bench facing the old sailing ship, the USS Constellation, she said, "Tell me about Frank."

"What do you want to know?"

"He's unusual."

"Like how?"

"He's insightful. And I get the feeling he's hooked into some kind of . . ." she shrugged. "I don't know. Paranormal pipeline most people can't access."

"Interesting you think so. Let me give you a little background. He returned from one of the Iraq wars with half a leg missing."

"The Iraq wars?"

He gave her a quick explanation.

"Okay. Back to Frank. I couldn't tell about the leg."

"Most people can't. I think something happened to him over there or when he was at the Naval Medical Center recovering. Something he doesn't talk about."

"So you don't think I'm right?"

"No I do. I think it's something he has to keep secret."

"Why?"

"Because none of us knows exactly where he lives or what he does when he's not at the office—or at conferences looking for new recruits. But one thing you can see, he looks a lot younger than his age."

"Which is what?"

"He's in his late fifties—at least."

"You're right. He doesn't look it."

Jonah was silent for several moments, then said. "Here's my crazy theory about Frank. When you were a kid, did you ever read the Narnia books?"

"Yes. I loved them."

"Then you know they were about kids who had adventures in another time continuum. They could be gone for years, but when they came back, they were no older than when they left."

"I remember."

"I think Frank goes somewhere like that. It's a good place for him. He's not married, but if I had to guess, I'd say he has a lover there. It could be a whole harem, but I think he's not that kind of guy."

"That's a lot of speculation."

He shifted in his seat. "Okay, here's *my* secret. For me, being a telepath means I'm always aware of people I care about. You. The other Decorah agents. Frank. I don't mean I eavesdrop on them or know exactly where they are—but they're part of the background in my head. And, um, when Frank goes away, he *goes away. He's not there.*"

"My God. Do you talk to the other guys about it?"

"No. We never discuss his private life because we don't want to jeopardize it for him."

"In your case, because you love him like a father."

He shot her a quick glance. "It's that obvious?"

"I know your emotions. I know he means a lot to you."

Jonah nodded. He had never put his feelings for Frank into words, but Alice's assessment made sense.

He reached for her hand. "He finds people who are misfits because of their special talents and brings them into the Decorah family. I'm thankful that he found me."

"Like you found me."

"Uh huh."

"What about your real father?" she asked.

He felt a pang of sadness—and anger. "He and my mom were killed by a drunk driver on the highway."

Her grip on his hand tightened. "I'm so sorry."

"I was already in college. I'd moved out of the house, but it was still hard. I went from being a kid—to taking care of myself pretty quickly."

"That sounds rough."

"I coped." He swallowed hard, refocusing on good memories. "Dad and I got along. He taught me how to fix cars—and we'd do stuff like camping and fishing."

"Good." She was silent for a moment, then asked, "What about your talent?"

"I didn't really recognize it when I was a kid. Actually, not until I got into police work, and I realized I could tell if people were lying to me. Which was why I got fed up with the department. There was a lot of lying in the administration—on a lot of levels."

"Oh."

"Lucky for me, Frank approached me at a conference. He recognized what I had, and when I joined Decorah, Grant and Mack spent a lot of time improving my skills."

They sat together, not needing to talk, and watched the tourists enjoy the crisp fall day. Finally he said, "We should do some grocery shopping."

They drove to a supermarket near his apartment, and the place was another surprise.

"So drugstores have stuff you'd find in a grocery. And groceries have stuff you'd find in a drugstore."

"Right. They both want to take advantage of one-stop shopping."

Alice pushed a cart up and down the aisles, marveling at the number of products and the variety of produce.

"A lot of this stuff isn't in season," she said as she picked up a box of strawberries. We have them on the farm, but only in the spring."

"They're shipped in from Latin America. Or somewhere else that is warmer than here. But the later it gets in the year, the less flavor they have."

She nodded. "So don't bother with them?"

"Right."

She reached for a bag of green beans. "These are already snapped."

"They want to make it convenient. What do you want for dinner?"

"That's a hard question, since I didn't get any choices for months. What if I said—pancakes with sautéed apples?"

He laughed. "Fine by me. Should we get pancake mix?"

"You don't need a mix. It's just flour, milk, butter, and eggs. And baking powder."

"If you say so."

"And we'll get some other stuff too. Like maybe ground beef and potatoes."

"Sure."

They bought the supplies they needed. As they cooked the simple dinner together, Alice kept glancing at Jonah.

"What?"

"I'm still coming to grips with how everything's changed.

"Yeah." His face clouded, and she knew where his thoughts had leaped.

We're not going to lose each other, she said.

She knew it might not be true. And that gave their love-making later an edge of desperation.

In the morning, Jonah checked on Teddy's progress, then said to Alice, "I should set up the hunt for the bodies."

"Can I help?"

"It's probably going to be a tedious process. Let me show you how to get into the Web, and you can prowl around on your own for a while. Don't get onto any porn sites—or you're likely to pick up a computer virus."

"I guess you'd better explain that."

After setting Alice up with his laptop, and giving her his cell number in case she ran into any problems, Jonah went to find Grant at the Decorah medical facility.

His friend looked up as he came in the door.

Jonah took a seat next to him at the front desk. "I suppose you know Alice and I are going to go back and try to save Hayward's other victims—by eliminating the sick bastard as he's scooping up the first woman."

"Frank told me. And he said you might need some help from me."

"Yeah. I've got Teddy working on trying to identify the victims through accounts of women whose bodies were never found. But we need more than that—like DNA evidence."

"They didn't have DNA evidence back in the fifties and sixties."

"No. But they had DNA we can use. You know; like all those ads on TV for finding your ancestry?"

Grant nodded.

"Well, if we get samples, we may be able to narrow down the victims better."

Grant gave Jonah a direct look. "You're thinking about going back to the estate and digging up the bodies."

"First we have to find them. We need to get a cadaver dog."

"And its handler. Which brings up the point that we can't just waltz in there and start poking around. Not with that local cop on the alert."

"We've got two choices. We can sneak in at night. Or we can string out the line we gave Officer Cooper." Jonah was thinking it through as he continued to speak. "But he was pretty pissy about our being there. If we asked for permission, we'd probably have to jump through a lot of hoops to search for the bodies and dig them up. That would take time. And we might never get permission."

"You have time. You could spend years on research."

"No, Alice and I are scared shitless, wondering if we're gonna screw up the timeline so we never meet."

Grant gave his friend a sympathetic look. "Right. I wasn't thinking. I guess we have to go in at night and risk getting ourselves and a dog handler arrested."

"Uh huh."

"We'd better start with the canine. Can you use a search and rescue dog? I know a guy who does that."

"Cadaver dogs are different. Search and rescue dogs are looking for living people who can be saved, and cadaver dogs are looking for the dead. They find them from the smell of a dead human drifting up through the earth."

"After more than fifty years?"

"As far as I know."

Jonah's gaze turned inward as he remembered the last time he and Grant had visited the property. "We'll have to make it clear to whoever goes with us that this is a stealth operation. Which may make it hard to find someone willing to do it."

He went off to call several people and groups who advertised cadaver dog services. Most were willing to work with Decorah Security but backed out when they heard the assignment was on private property and had to be secret.

After making six calls, he found a guy named Doug Frampton, from Carol County, who was intrigued enough to keep listening.

"Why does it have to be covert?" he asked.

"We're investigating serial murders that occurred fifty years ago. The bodies are buried on an estate where the ownership is in dispute. We went there a few days ago, and a cop was instantly on our asses. We left, but we want to come back at night."

"You're sure the bodies are there?"

"It makes sense. The killer was kidnapping young women, forcing them to get into great physical shape, then hunting them for sport on the estate. It's a big place. He had plenty of room to use the grounds as a private cemetery."

Frampton winced. "Okay I'll join you. When do you want to do it?"

"As soon as possible."

"I can bring Daisy to your place tonight."

"Your dog is Daisy?"

"Yeah, I named her after my grandmother. She was dogged in pursuit of buried bodies. In the metaphorical sense, of course."

Jonah laughed, then gave Frampton directions. He proposed leaving in an SUV just before dark—which would put them at the estate around eight.

He headed home around 5:30 and found Alice in the kitchen, proudly taking a meatloaf out of the oven. To go along with it, she had made mashed potatoes, using the immersion blender she found in one of Jonah's cabinets.

"That was a Christmas present that I never used," he said.

"I looked it up on the Web. It's fun."

"You don't have to do all the cooking."

"I like it. It's a lot easier than when my mom did it. I mean, you just put that wand right into the pot where you cooked the potatoes, add butter, milk and salt, and mash them up."

He shook his head. "You're adapting pretty well."

The tone of his voice must have told her something was up.

"What?"

"After dinner, Grant and I are going out to the estate—with a cadaver dog and handler."

"I want to come," she said at once.

"I knew you'd say that, but in this case, it's better if you stay here."

"Why?"

"Because the morning I came to the estate looking for you—a cop showed up and was pretty aggressive. He could come back, and the fewer people we have, the better."

"You and Grant are both going."

"We'll be on gravedigger duty. Do you really want to dig up long-dead bodies?"

She winced. "If you put it that way—no."

As he got ready to go to the Decorah office, she reached for him. "Be careful."

"I will."

"Won't the cop see your flashlights?"

He shook his head. "Another modern invention you don't know about—night vision goggles. You can see pretty well in the dark with them. Of course, everything looks green, but you get used to it."

Before he left, they hugged tightly because both of them now knew that every step they took toward fulfilling their mission could mean they'd end up separated forever.

〜

When Jonah arrived at the office, Frampton and a handsome black and brown shepherd were in the office waiting room, talking to Frank.

The handler was a man who looked to be in his late fifties or early sixties, and Jonah wondered briefly if he would be up to the assignment—physically. But he was the only one who had agreed to take the job.

The team, including the dog, piled into an SUV and headed for the Bay Bridge. On the way, Frampton asked questions about the case.

"How did you find out about a bunch of bodies from fifty years ago?"

Jonah kept himself from glancing at Grant. He couldn't tell the dog handler the truth—that he'd time-traveled back to the scene of the crimes.

He settled on saying, "We got the information from a source who has to remain anonymous."

"But you think the info is reliable?"

"We wouldn't risk getting caught by the local cops if we didn't," Grant answered.

That kept Frampton quiet for a few miles before he asked, "Do you know anything about the victims?"

"We're trying to find out more. That's why we want to locate the bodies. We're assuming they are all young woman, probably in their early twenties."

"You often take cases this complicated?"

"Not usually. But this is special."

Jonah was relieved when they drew near to the estate and he could focus on looking for the spot where he had parked the night of the fire. He drove down the road once with his lights on, then switched them off and came back, slowing as he reached the dirt turnoff. Pulling off the blacktop, he headed for the edge of the woods, then stopped near where he'd parked the Chevy.

They all got out, and Frampton let Daisy get used to the environment. As it turned out, the moon was almost full, and they didn't need the night vision goggles to walk the property.

"Do you know where the remains might be?" the dog handler asked.

"I wish I did," Jonah answered. "I assume his graveyard's not too far from the house for him to carry the women over."

"Do you think the killer would want to see the graveyard from the window?"

Jonah considered what he knew about the man. "That's a good possibility."

"We can get closer to the house and start walking a grid."

Jonah didn't have a better suggestion. He and Grant held back, letting the man and dog do their work.

After two hours, Frampton and Daisy were still going, and Jonah was surprised at the man's willingness to push himself. He was thinking they might have to come back another night when the dog stopped and alerted on a patch of ground about two hundred yards from the river and about the same distance from the house.

While Frampton rewarded Daisy with praise and dog treats, the Decorah agents went back to the SUV for their shovels and the goggles so they'd be able to see fine details and wouldn't dig right through a decomposed body. Working carefully, they began poking around in the now hardened ground.

"I think the graves won't be more than a few feet down," Frampton said as he and Daisy withdrew to let the agents work.

Jonah was the first to feel his shovel blade hit what was either a small rock or bone. He and Grant switched to trowels and began scooping earth away. After a few minutes, they uncovered a pelvic bone.

The dog came leaping over, and Frampton had to restrain her.

They collected a DNA sample from the bone, then began looking for more.

"I can help," Frampton said.

"Appreciate it."

After taking the dog back to the vehicle, he joined the Decorah agents in the digging.

With all three working, it took only another couple of hours to find the five victims and to bag samples.

They were just heading back to the car when Daisy started barking furiously.

CHAPTER NINETEEN

"Christ, what's that?" Jonah muttered.

The words were hardly out of his mouth when a powerful flashlight beam hit him in the face.

"Hands in the air, don't move."

The three men froze.

Jonah recognized the voice. It was Officer Daniels, the cop who had chased them off the estate the first time. He must have spotted something going on over here, turned off his lights, and crept up on the action.

"What the hell are you doing?" he asked.

To his companions Jonah said in a low voice, "Watch it. This guy is trigger happy." To the cop, he said, "We're unarmed. We came back to look for the bodies I told you about."

"Unarmed?" The cop had a dilemma now. He had three suspects who might be up to no good, but he couldn't search them because while he was busy with one guy, the others might get the drop on him.

"How do you know about any bodies?" he demanded. What he should have done was call for immediate backup, Jonah thought, but he wasn't going to make helpful suggestions.

Jonah had been mulling over an answer to that question all evening. Now he said, "The granddaughter of one of the victims always suspected that Arthur Hayward was responsible for her grandmother's disappearance. She hired Decorah Security to see if we could find the body and prove what had happened."

"You said five bodies."

"Our research told us there were likely five victims."

"That sounds like a cock and bull story. You got a guard dog in the vehicle. What are you here to steal?"

"Nothing," Frampton answered.

"And who the hell are you?"

"I am Douglas Frampton, a licensed cadaver dog handler. The animal in the vehicle is not a guard dog. She locates human remains, and she found five bodies on this property."

"Prove it."

"We can take you to the graves," Jonah said.

"Yeah, because you put the stiffs there," Daniels said.

Jonah suspected the response meant the guy wasn't going to release them now. This small-town cop was such a dick that Jonah wanted to scream, but he kept his voice even. "I told you last time. These are cold cases. The women disappeared in the late fifties or early sixties. I wasn't born then."

"Nor was I," Grant added.

"And I was a toddler," Frampton said. "The remains are completely skeletonized. We reburied them."

"Why?"

"To keep predators from getting to them," Jonah answered.

"We'll have a look at the graves in the morning," Daniels snapped. "Meanwhile, you three are under arrest for trespassing."

"Jesus," Jonah muttered under his breath.

"What's that?"

"Nothing."

"What about my dog?" Frampton asked.

"She'll be taken to the pound."

Frampton looked like he wanted to lunge at the cop, but Jonah shook his head.

"Don't do it."

"Better listen to him," Daniels growled.

"Can we make a call to our boss?" Jonah asked.

"In the morning."

Frustration pounded through Jonah, until he remembered he didn't need a phone to make a call. He sent his thoughts outward.

Alice. Are you there? Alice.

She answered instantly, *Yes,* and he knew she had been anxiously waiting for him to give her some news.

Did you find the other victims?

Yes. But we've got a problem. The dickhead cop is back and wants to arrest us and take the cadaver dog to the pound.

Dickhead?

I'll explain that later. Call Frank and let him know the situation.

Okay. Right away.

He felt the connection between them grow fuzzy because she was shifting her attention to the phone.

A few moments later, she asked, *Where are you?*

Jonah looked at the cop. "Where are you taking us?"

"To the Kent County jail."

He conveyed the information to Alice.

"You won't at least look at the graves while we're here?" Jonah asked.

"No."

They had to wait for transportation and also for animal control to collect Daisy. Then they were finally searched, and

Daniels took away the messenger bag in which Jonah had stowed the five samples they'd collected from the victims.

Shoved into two separate patrol cars, they were driven to the Kent County government complex.

By the time they arrived, a helicopter was sitting on the nearby landing pad.

Frank Decorah, wearing a beautifully tailored suit, got out and strode toward the lead car. He was followed by a man in a similar business outfit. Jonah recognized him as the high-powered lawyer named Spencer Cortez, whom Decorah kept on retainer.

Daniels jumped out of his black and white and faced the newcomers. "Who are you?"

"Frank Decorah, the head of Decorah Security. I sent these men to investigate the murders Jonah Ranger told you about."

The cop stuck out his chin. "And how did you know to come here?"

"We were afraid something like this might happen, and we were monitoring your communications," Frank replied smoothly.

Good answer, Jonah thought. Or maybe it was true.

Daniels turned to the cop who had driven the second squad car. "I can handle this."

The other guy looked doubtful, and Daniels said, "Go in and wait for me."

When the fifth wheel had complied, Daniels said, "These men were trespassing on private property—in the middle of the night."

Cortez stepped forward. "I understand that you were informed earlier that there might be remains of murder victims on the Hayward property."

"Why should I have believed that?" Daniels shot back.

"There are plenty of reasons these guys could have been trespassing."

"And you chose to assume they were lying about the bodies," the lawyer countered. "If you persist in holding these men for participating in a legitimate investigation, we will sue you and Kent County for twenty million dollars."

Daniels' jaw dropped. "That's outrageous. They were on private property. Your nuisance suit will be dismissed."

"And appealed. And the press will get an earful about how you wanted to block a murder investigation. I think we have a good case, and I think the county administration will not thank you for stopping these men from identifying murder victims."

In the face of all the negative information, Jonah could see that the cop didn't know what to do.

"If you let these men go now, Decorah Security will make a generous $50,000 contribution to the county police fund."

From the corner of his eye Jonah saw a black SUV drive slowly into the parking lot and pull up several yards away. But his attention snapped back to the confrontation as Daniels said, "Are you trying to bribe me?"

"Of course not. I'm giving you a way to make this a win-win situation. In the morning, the men will show you where to find the bodies. But right now we want to take the DNA samples back to Decorah Security so we can get started on the identification as soon as possible. And, of course, if we find out who the victims are, we will share the information with you."

Daniels sighed. "Okay, I'm willing to let them go tonight, provided they are available in the morning to show my department the graves."

"Fair enough," the lawyer answered. "Since it's already rather late, why don't you make it 11:00 am?"

"I've arranged accommodations for them at the Hilton Garden Inn," Frank said.

"What about my dog?" Frampton asked.

"You can pick her up at Animal Control in the morning."

"She'd better be all right."

Before Daniels could turn away, Frank said, "Give us the bag with the DNA samples so we can get started."

The cop gave Frank a narrow-eyed look but handed over the bag before turning and stomping into the building.

"Thanks," Jonah said to Frank.

"No problem. And you got what you were looking for?"

"Yes. Did you really monitor their communications?"

"No. Alice called Decorah—and they got me."

The passenger door of the SUV that had arrived late opened. Alice climbed out and ran to Jonah. He caught her and hugged her to him.

"Good going."

"I was scared for you," she whispered.

"But you did exactly the right thing."

When the driver's door opened, Grant's wife Jen joined the group and was introduced to Frampton.

Frank looked at the two couples and the dog handler. "Good job. In the morning, you can take Doubting Thomas over and show him the graves."

CHAPTER TWENTY

Jen reset the GPS for the short drive to the hotel.

"I can't believe that thing tells you where to go," Alice said.

"Better than a map," Jonah told her. "Unless it screws up. That does happen."

A sleepy-looking desk clerk checked them in, and they headed for their various rooms. Once Jonah had closed the door behind them, Alice reached for him and held tight.

After a few moments, he murmured, "Let me take a shower before we go any further. We've been digging up graves."

"Oh—right."

He stepped into the bathroom and closed the door. When she heard the shower running, she took off her own clothes and followed him under the hot running water.

He turned in surprise, then grinned when he saw her. "Well, this is a nice surprise."

"I think you deserve a little treat," she answered. Reaching for the soap, she lathered her hands, then began working on his chest, paying particular attention to his nipples. By the time she reached his cock he was already rock hard. She clasped him tightly, using her soap-slick hand to slide up and down his length, stroking him the way he had showed her.

"You're going to make me come," he gasped out.

"Uh huh."

She kept pleasuring him, reveling in his shout of satisfaction when he climaxed. He leaned against the wall, catching his breath.

"So you were going to tell me—what's a dickhead?"

"I think you can probably guess."

"Would it be like a cockhead?"

He laughed. "You're a quick learner." His eyes roamed over her body "And now you."

"Well, maybe you can—you know—dry me off and fuck me."

"Fuck you? Where did you pick that up?"

"A cable TV show. And yes, my mom would have washed my mouth out with soap if she'd heard me say it."

He turned off the water and reached for a big fluffy towel, which he used to dry her and turn both of them on at the same time.

Neither of them could walk the few yards to the bed. Instead, he sat down on the toilet lid and pulled her down on his cock.

She stayed there, unmoving, for several long seconds, looking down into his upturned face.

But when he sucked one of her nipples into his mouth and began to play with it, she had to respond.

She rode him like the magnificent man he was, pressing her clit against him, giving herself maximum stimulation, climbing higher on a spiral of pleasure. And when she came, she felt him follow her.

They clung together, kissing and stroking each other. As the bathroom started to cool, he carried her to bed, and they snuggled together.

She closed her eyes, clinging to him, praying that everything would work out so that they could be together forever.

Forever, he echoed her thought. And she knew he had her.

The next morning, Frampton collected his dog, who was none the worse for her stay at the pound. The women dropped the search team back at their car and returned to Beltsville. The three men took Officer Daniels back to the estate and showed him the graves. After that, there was a lot of activity as the medical examiner was notified—which meant the remains would go to Baltimore where all Maryland autopsies were handled.

By the time Jonah and Grant returned to the office, Frank had already submitted the samples for expedited DNA, and Teddy Granada was moving ahead with the public records.

It took a few weeks to get a final list of victims.

Frank and Jonah called in Alice when they had the names.

Her stomach was churning as she joined them in one of the computer rooms.

"Okay," Teddy Granada said. "The whole thing has been a massive effort of detective work. But we're 99 percent certain we've identified the five women Hayward took—using contemporary accounts and the DNA. We've got Lisa Sams, Karen Anderson, Beth Jorgenson, Paula Hammond, and Jean Shombert."

The names gave Alice a jolt. Before this, they had just been victims. Now they were real women

"And what do you know about them?" she asked.

"I don't want to minimize them, but as far as we can tell,

they were all pretty ordinary," Teddy began. "Except for their athletic abilities. But none of them was training for an Olympic team."

Alice glared at him. "Put me in that category. I was ordinary."

"Of course not!" Jonah objected.

"I was a farm girl who was into 4H and good at sports. Being 'ordinary' was probably part of his reason for taking me. But each of them was special if you go into the details of her life."

"Okay, yeah," Teddy agreed.

"And he's not going to get them. We can stop him." Alice reached for Jonah's hand and clasped it tightly.

The look in his eyes made her want to weep. She saw his pride in her, but also his panic at the thought of losing her. They were acting like this was going to be an easy fix. In reality, all their hopes and dreams for a life together could vaporize in an instant. Yet neither one of them could turn away from the road they had started down.

"Where was the first abduction?" Alice asked.

"Just across the Pennsylvania line in Garrison, Pennsylvania. There was a flood, and Lisa Sams was supposedly swept away. Her body was never recovered."

"He used a flood?" she asked, hardly able to believe it.

"I guess he knew from the weather reports that it was coming, and he went up there and scooped her up."

Frank looked at Jonah. "And you think you can get there—in solid enough form to stop Hayward?"

"I hope I can."

Her eyes shot daggers at him. "What do you mean—I? I assumed we were going together. We're you just stringing me along?"

"I'm hoping you see reason. This is too dangerous for you," he snapped, letting her know how much he was on edge.

Alice wasn't going to give in. "We're not really rescuing her from a flood. We're rescuing her from Hayward."

They glared at each other, Alice determined to go, and Jonah determined to handle it alone.

The stalemate was broken by Frank, who said, "She's right. You'll have a better chance if Alice is with you. One of you needs to grab the girl, and the other needs to take care of Hayward."

Alice knew Jonah would defer to Frank. "I guess I'm outnumbered."

"And there's another reason she has to be with you," Frank said. "We don't know what will happen to her after you stop the first abduction and she's no longer dead as far as the world is concerned. To be safe, the two of you will have to get to the scene of the rock slide pretty quickly."

They spent the next two weeks doggedly practicing the time-travel techniques that they were going to need.

Still, as they drove north in Alice's old Chevy, Jonah couldn't help thinking the mission was insane.

But he did get a sense of calm from the vehicle. It had been the original bridge between himself and Alice

He knew she sensed his thoughts when she reached over and laid her hand on his thigh.

I love you, she whispered in his mind. *You didn't have to do this. But here you are.*

I love you too. That's why I didn't want you in danger again, he answered.

I know. I wish I'd never thought of doing this.

But as soon as you did, we both knew we had to save them.

Before leaving, they had collected as much information as

possible on Lisa Sams—including a smiling black and white photo that had been circulated when she'd gone missing in the flood. She was blond with light eyes—apparently the type Hayward liked. She'd been a nursing student at the University of Maryland and had gone on a camping trip with her family just after her junior year. Probably the killer had been keeping track of her for some time.

Jonah and Alice had read newspaper accounts of the tragedy and formed a theory of what had happened that day. The family had been packing up their campsite to get away from the rising torrent in Sweet Water Creek when their dog had run off. The animal had come back, but nobody had ever seen Lisa again—except Arthur Hayward. The killer had probably lured the animal away with food, then maybe he made it squeal in pain—sending Lisa after it, so that Hayward could grab her and slip away. He could have been another camper fleeing from the flooding creek.

As they drove into the small town of Timberton, they went over details of their plan. Jonah had worked out a strategy that he hoped would do the trick. He'd practiced the technique over and over. But he'd never used it to take down a killer.

The bright sunshine was disconcerting when they knew they'd soon be heading into a thunderous rainstorm.

Once they'd figured out the victim and the location, they'd done more research and found out Arthur Hayward had stayed in the Plum Tree Motel, which had long since been torn down and replaced by a strip shopping center. But large tracts of land in and around the town were still undeveloped including the site of the campground.

Jonah pulled into a wooded area near the shopping center. The creek was still there, a small stream running between deeply eroded banks.

Alice stared at the placidly flowing water. "It's hard to believe that little creek got big enough to flood the area."

"Well, the newspapers said it came raging over its banks taking Lisa and several other people with it. And from there, anything in the water was swept into the Green River."

As Jonah cut the engine, he was thinking his mission was more complicated than it had been when Alice had called out to him. She'd drawn him to her. Now he had to arrive at the right time and place on his own. But he was almost certain he could do it. He'd practiced enough, picking specific times and out-of-the-way places.

They got out of the car, opened the trunk and took out the rain gear they'd bought at an outfitter store, waterproof jackets and pants that were more modern and lightweight than what had been available in the fifties.

Luckily, there didn't seem to be anyone else around as they headed into the woods.

Moment of truth, Alice said silently as they moved between the trees, into a spot where they couldn't easily be seen.

Jonah nodded and reached for her. She came into his arms, clinging tightly, partly because the close contact was necessary for the process of taking her along and partly because they were both aware of the danger. They were going to confront a killer. And because they were taking him out long before he had abducted Alice, they were both thinking about what could happen to her.

Jonah folded her close, his whole body tensing as he strove to get this right. Closing his eyes, he let the raging water of the creek flow into his mind as he pictured the long-ago scene.

The newspaper article had included the time when Lisa had disappeared, which gave him another focus.

Even though he knew where and when he was going, he struggled with resistance. The drag on his time travel ability was unfortunately Alice. It was easier to go back alone, but after considering Frank's assessment, he knew he had to take her with him. If the killer wasn't around to abduct her, then she was still alive in the future—which created a time paradox. Time paradoxes were the reason he hadn't come here on his own to check out the location. He couldn't take a chance of two of him being in the same place at the same time.

Right, she said, and he could feel her trying to change the time-travel equation—adding power rather than taking it away.

She hadn't tried to do it in their practice sessions, but now he knew she was striving to add the force of her will to his mind.

He felt a kind of mental warm glow, like hot fudge on a sundae, as he sensed that she was boosting his power. Her added mental energy pushed him over the top, and all at once they were at the location in the past—with water pounding down on the hood of his rain jacket.

His eyes blinked open as he took in the deluge.

He had been prepared for a downpour, but not like *this.* Water pouring out of the sky in sheets so thick and fast that he could barely see—or breathe. And the downpour was so heavy, it was almost impossible to make out Alice standing next to him. If he couldn't see someone a foot away, how were they going to find Lisa or Hayward?

As that thought flashed through his mind, the rain eased up a little.

They looked around to get their bearings. At first they saw only the scattered debris of campers' hasty departures. The flood warnings had already sent most of the families packing in a hurry. The smart ones, Jonah thought.

Could we have gotten the time wrong? Could Lisa's family have left? Alice asked.

Not according to the newspaper article.

They should be here. But where?

Jonah and Alice sloshed through puddles, looking for the Samses. The campground was divided into sections, each with its own electrical hookup. Finally, through the rain, he spotted movement that wasn't falling water and gestured toward the right. They hurried as fast as they could in that direction and came out in a clearing where a man, woman and a couple of kids were frantically trying to pack up a wet tent.

There's Lisa. Alice pointed to a young woman wearing a yellow slicker. She had no hat, and her blond hair was plastered to her head.

She pulled out a pet carrier and tried to stuff a sopping wet animal inside.

The dog. It wiggled out of her grasp and took off into the downpour in the direction of the river.

"Snowball, come back here. Snowball, bad dog. Come back here," she wailed.

At least that was a piece of luck. They could follow the animal—hoping it would lead them to Hayward.

The girl was about to go after the dog when a cop car with flashing lights drove into the clearing.

A trooper in rain gear climbed out and stomped over to Mr. Sams.

"Sir, you're supposed to be out of here."

The father turned toward the officer. "We're trying to pack up."

"You should have been gone an hour ago. I ought to give you a citation."

The father's voice quavered. "I'm sorry. We're going."

The officer gave him one more long look, then turned away and spotted Jonah and Alice. "And what the hell are you doing here?" he asked.

"We're reporters for the Garrison Times," Jonah said, remembering the name of the local paper.

"Oh yeah; well you know this area is off limits." He looked around. "Where's your vehicle?"

Jonah gestured, "in the woods."

"Get back there and get out of here."

The only thing they could do was follow directions, feeling the officer's eyes on them.

Finally, he got back into his cruiser and backed up, sending mud flying into the air. On the access road, he splashed up water as he hit a series of potholes.

At the Sams camp spot, Lisa was weeping. "I have to get Snowball."

"That police officer told us to leave," her father said.

The girl stared at him for a long moment. "No."

The father made a grab for her, but she dodged away and took off, running in the direction where the dog had disappeared.

They heard her father curse and yell after her.

He's gonna see us if we follow her, Alice shouted in his mind.

Yeah, Jonah answered. They separated and circled around, finally heading in the direction the girl had taken but staying twenty yards apart.

At first Jonah had no idea where the young woman had gone. Then he heard Lisa calling the pup's name, her voice breaking as she made one more try to get her pet back.

There was no response until they heard a series of yelps over the sound of the rain and the rushing water.

"Snowball!"

Lisa ducked around some brambles, and followed the increasingly frantic yelps.

Jonah and Alice had talked about how to handle this. Following their plan, they stayed separated, one going left and the other right, each of them heading for the other side of the thicket.

Jonah came out first and saw a man, dressed in a black rain jacket and dark pants. He was holding the dog, squeezing him painfully. Lisa was standing a few yards away crying. "Stop hurting him. Give him to me," she pleaded.

"Come and get him."

The girl was cautious. She could see that this man was dangerous, but she wanted her pet returned unharmed.

She inched closer, and as she got within grabbing distance, Hayward tossed the dog down and reached for her, one of his big hands closing around her arm and his other hand clamping over her mouth.

As Snowball streaked away, she struggled, but to no avail.

Jonah came up on the killer's right.

Sensing movement, the man looked up, his features hardening as he saw someone interfering with his plans.

"Let her go," Jonah called out.

"Who the hell are you?"

"Your worst nightmare," Jonah answered.

With one hand around the girl's throat, Hayward whipped out a gun and held it to her temple as he pulled her against his chest.

She whimpered.

"Shut up," Hayward ordered, before looking directly at Jonah. "Stay back. I'll kill the little bitch if you come any closer."

CHAPTER TWENTY-ONE

Jonah stopped in his tracks, unable to take a risk that the man would follow through on his threat.

To his left, Alice stepped into view.

"Take me instead," she called over the pounding of the rain.

The serial killer shifted slightly, peering at her. "Do I know you?"

"Not yet."

"What the hell does that mean?"

"I guess you'll find out."

"Stay back, or the girl dies," Hayward warned again.

"Okay," Jonah called out. "Take it easy."

As Hayward shifted back to him, something happened that the kidnapper could never have anticipated.

Jonah vanished.

"What the fuck?" Hayward stared blankly at the spot where Jonah had been standing.

The killer took the gun away from the girl's neck, waving it around at chest level as he tried to figure out where the man had gone.

Seconds later, Jonah appeared behind the killer scuffing his feet in the wet leaves.

Taken completely by surprise, Hayward whirled, letting go of the girl as he leveled the gun at Jonah. But suddenly his nemesis wasn't there again.

"Run," Alice shouted to the girl.

She didn't need a further invitation and took off back the way she'd come. From the woods, the dog joined her.

The kidnapper's gun was now aimed at Alice.

She kept her gaze steady. "Kill me and you won't have anyone to put in that cell under your mansion."

He goggled at her. "What? How could you know about that?"

"Because I was there, and I escaped."

"Impossible. This girl is my first."

"She would have been."

Before Hayward could formulate an answer, Jonah appeared behind him again, pulling up his gun hand. The weapon discharged, but it probably sounded like a clap of thunder in the rain. Jonah twisted the arm. The man screamed as a bone cracked, and he dropped the weapon.

Alice swooped in and kicked the revolver away, then delivered a kick to Hayward's balls.

He screamed and doubled over.

"I'd love to draw this out and give you a nice long beating, but I'm afraid we don't have time," Alice said.

Jonah chopped at the man's neck and he went down.

They each picked him up with a hand under an armpit and dragged him toward the rushing water.

With a mighty heave, they tossed him in. The cold water woke him up, and he screamed as the swollen creek carried him away. Jonah saw a log strike his head, and he went under the surface.

They could hear running feet behind them and both whirled. A big man was coming toward them—fast—holding an ax. It was Lisa's father.

He lowered the weapon when he saw them but still looked wary.

"Are you the two people who saved my daughter?"

"Yes," Alice answered, swiping water out of her face.

He gazed around, staring into the rain. "Where is the guy?"

Jonah gestured toward the water. "He slipped and fell in."

"He did?"

"Yeah. And you'd better get out of here before that cop comes back and gives you a citation." Jonah took Alice's arm, and they started back the way they'd come.

"Wait. Who are you?"

"Nobody," Jonah called over his shoulder. "Finish packing and get out of here before the water rises any farther and your whole family gets washed away."

Without waiting for an answer, they walked rapidly through the woods. When they were out of sight and sure the father wasn't following them, they embraced, just standing there for long moments.

"We got him," Alice said, sounding like she could hardly believe they had done it.

"Thank God. But we'd better leave."

Jonah reversed the process. Once again, Alice added mental energy, and he easily took them back to where they had started —only a few yards farther from the car.

Alice blinked in the sunlight. "Thank God," she breathed.

Jonah tightened his grip on her, stroking his hands up and down her body, thankful that she was still in his arms. In truth, he hadn't known if she would vanish after the killer was eliminated.

Lowering his mouth, he gave her a long, passionate kiss, and she responded with equal heat.

"Too bad we don't have time to celebrate," she said, when he finally lifted his head.

"Later."

She grinned at him. "Those short time hops you practiced really paid off,"

"I was hoping they would give us the edge."

"We should get on to the next project." As she turned toward the car, she wavered on her feet, and he gripped her arm.

"Are you okay?"

Alice swallowed hard and gave the only answer she could, "Yes."

"Good girl. I know you're shaky, which is all the more reason to finish this thing quickly."

"You mean because Hayward is dead, and the clock is ticking for me?" she said with a little hitch in her voice.

She was sure he wanted to deny the danger to her, but he wasn't going to lie.

"Exactly."

They returned to the car, quickly stripped off their rain gear and tossed it in the trunk. Now they were wearing jeans and tee shirts suitable for the current weather conditions.

Alice leaned back in her seat and closed her eyes.

"You don't feel well?"

"I feel weighted down," she replied.

"Can you be a little clearer?"

"Like it's hard to lift my arms and legs. And hard to breathe," she admitted.

～

Fear sizzled through Jonah. He thanked God that Alice hadn't vanished in a flash. But he knew time was starting to crowd her out of existence because Hayward was now dead. How long did she have?

The only certainty was that they'd better hurry.

She closed her eyes and lolled against the seat while they headed for Western Maryland.

As he drove, it was tempting to speed—like an escaped soul fleeing from hell. But he ordered himself not to press the accelerator to the floor. He was thankful that this part of Pennsylvania was close to the place where Alice had been abducted, and he breathed a sigh of relief when she opened her eyes and started looking out the window.

"Almost there," she said, pointing to a gravel road. "That's the turnoff to the camp."

He'd visited the place the week before and knew the camp was out of business. When they reached the location, he saw only the dilapidated buildings that had lasted into the current century.

He also knew where Hayward had staged the fake accident because the rock slide was still there. It was a gigantic pile of boulders that would have been impossible to move without heavy equipment.

He kept driving, until the road became too narrow to navigate. From the look of fatigue on Alice's face, he hoped she could make it to the right spot.

"I used to come up this way a lot," she said, her voice barely above a whisper. "I loved the peace and quiet. I didn't know a killer was paying attention to my habits."

"Yeah. Back in the early sixties nobody expected to go out for a hike and get snatched. You stay here. I'll go investigate." Fear had him jogging up the trail through trees with almost bare branches. He had gone perhaps two hundred yards when he saw the spot where a cliff had collapsed.

And to his relief, nobody was around.

"Thank God," he breathed as he turned and jogged back.

Alice was sitting with her eyes closed, but they drifted open when she heard him.

"I found it. Nobody's here."

She pushed herself up. "We'd better hurry."

"Yeah," he answered. Theoretically they had all the time in the world—but not for Alice.

From the trunk, he collected supplies he hadn't needed at the campground. After shouldering a backpack, he put his arm around Alice, helping her walk up the trail.

He could hear her labored breathing and feel her faltering steps.

Please, God, he silently prayed. *Let me get her there in time.*

I heard that.

He laughed, then said aloud, "It's gonna be okay. I'm just nervous."

After that, he tried to keep his thoughts on the task ahead, but there was no way he could keep panic from drifting into the edges of his mind.

When he heard her gasp, alarm grabbed him again. But she was only reacting to the enormous pile of rocks.

"Oh Lord. No wonder they didn't try to find me."

"We'll put everything right," he said, quickly switching his thoughts to the date and time—which they knew from the newspaper articles they'd read.

They were so close. So close to finishing this. But as he started the process of taking them back to 1961, he could feel the weakness of Alice's energy level.

Desperately, he expended his own life force to push them back to the date she'd been taken.

They had left on a crisp fall day. They materialized into late summer, with leafy trees and chirping birds. Alice looked around and shuddered.

He tried again to gauge her health. "Are you okay?"

"Yes. It looks so pretty in summer, but this was the worst day of my life."

"We'll change that. Hayward isn't here now."

"But he captured the old me, and we're going to scare the shit out of her anyway."

"I'm sorry."

It all seemed so unreal, Alice thought as she fought not to be sick.

"Come on. Come on," she heard Jonah mutter as they lurked in the shadows, waiting for the old Alice to come up the trail. He kept glancing at his watch, the seconds ticking by.

"Could it be the wrong time?" he finally asked.

"I don't think so," she answered, although now she wasn't sure.

"Should we try again and pick another time in the afternoon?"

She dragged in a breath and let it out, before whispering what neither one of them wanted to hear. "No, I don't think I could survive another time jump."

"Christ."

"We have to wait."

She knew he wanted to *do something*. But all he could do was help her to sit down on the mossy ground and sling his arm around her, pulling her close.

Leaning her head on his shoulder, she closed her eyes and drifted in some region of reality that she couldn't name. She loved this man, and this might be the last time they sat together.

"No," he said aloud, and she knew he had picked up on her thoughts. Trying to simply enjoy this time with him, she reached for his hand and felt his fingers close around hers.

She wasn't sure how long they sat there in the shade of the trees, but finally she felt him tense.

A sizzle of alarm shot through her, and her eyes blinked open. Despite knowing Hayward had been swept away by the rushing water, she couldn't stop herself from expecting him here. But it wasn't Hayward.

Here she is.

She saw a woman dressed in shorts and a tee shirt come up the trail. For a startled moment, she thought it wasn't her. If you counted the time she'd been in captivity and then when she'd been living with Jonah, only a few months had passed since this moment. But she was astonished at how different she looked.

"Wimpy," was the word she'd use—after all the physical training she'd been forced to endure. It wasn't just that. She'd lived in Jonah's decade for less than a month, but the new reality had definitely changed her. Plus, she'd kept up an exercise routine because she liked the way it made her feel.

Jonah got up, moving rapidly through the trees. He came up from behind Alice's old self and grabbed her, clamping a hand over her mouth as he dragged her off the trail.

Although she struggled, she was no match for a Decorah Security agent.

Alice felt her stomach lurch as she watched Jonah carry the figure away, toward the thick grove of trees.

When they came close, Alice saw the panic in the girl's eyes. They widened as they darted to the waiting woman, taking in the familiar features.

Alice wanted to say something reassuring.

Jonah was in too much of a hurry. He pulled a cloth from a small ziplock bag and pressed the ether-soaked fabric to the girl's nose and mouth. As she lost consciousness, he eased her to the ground.

"Stay with her," he said, getting out equipment he'd taken from the car.

Alice clenched her teeth as she moved closer to her former self.

She was feeling sicker by the minute, but she knew there was no help for it until Jonah finished with his job.

He'd studied the cliff—both before and after Hayward's blast. And he'd talked to experts about the best places to set the charges.

She knew Hayward had had time to arrange the accident. Probably he'd set the charges days earlier. Jonah didn't have that luxury because he couldn't take a chance on someone else getting hurt.

She watched him expertly climb the face of the cliff. When he reached a spot near the top, he took off his backpack, removed some of the plastic explosives he'd brought, and began wedging the charges deep into crevices.

Alice glanced down at her old self, reaching a hand to stroke her arm. It felt comforting to touch this woman who was part of her—but not.

She was starting to feel dizzy. She'd been fighting the sick feeling since they'd left the campgrounds. Now it was almost impossible to push through the weakness.

Unable to sit any longer, she fell to the side. From that odd angle, she saw Jonah glance toward her in alarm.

Alice?

I think I'm fading away, she managed to say. *I guess me and my shadow can't be in the same place at the same time. And I'm the one who doesn't belong.*

Oh Christ!

As her head swam, she saw Jonah hurry with what he was doing—probably not working carefully enough. Then he scrambled down the cliff face. Dropping to the ground, he came running toward her.

"Let him get away in time. Let him get away in time," she chanted over and over as she watched him putting distance between himself and the huge rock formation.

He was almost out of range when a low blast broke off huge chunks of the cliff.

Smaller pieces rained down on his running figure, and she gasped as she saw him stumble. When a couple of enormous boulders broke loose and rolled toward him, she cried out.

It looked like they were going to overtake him—until he put on a burst of speed.

He was still pelting toward her. He had saved himself. But it was too late for her.

She could barely breathe now. Barely think. Barely feel the ground under her body.

She thought she heard Jonah calling her name. But she wasn't sure because every sense had dimmed.

Jonah was speaking but the words didn't reach her. He must have known because he knelt beside her and shouted directly into her mind, *Hold . . . your double,* he said urgently. *The way we do when we time travel. Hold her and make yourself one with her.*

She understood what he wanted, but it was hard to even lift her arms.

Let me help you.

She felt Jonah turn her and use his body to press her down, holding and pushing her against the other Alice. As he did, he tightened his grip on the two of them.

It was so strange. She knew he was pressing hard, but she

could barely feel him. Barely feel anything. She was so tired it was impossible to hold her eyes open. She felt Jonah pouring energy into her, and she struggled to grab on to it as she tried to hold on to the woman who was also herself.

That was confusing, she thought, just before she felt herself losing consciousness and heard Jonah desperately calling her name.

I love you, she managed to say as everything went black.

CHAPTER TWENTY-TWO

It might have been minutes later—or hours—when she felt Jonah's hand clasping hers as his thumb pressed and rubbed against her palm.

Her eyes blinked open and she stared up into his dear, familiar face, seeing the lines of worry and fear etched there.

Alice, he asked urgently, *Is it you? Do you know me?*

She smiled at the question. It might have sounded strange, but she knew what he meant. She had been fading out of existence since they'd pitched Hayward into the rushing river. Then they'd gone back to stage the accident that had supposedly buried her earlier self. But only one Alice could survive, and Jonah didn't yet know which one it was.

Yes. It's me. And I know who you are—the man I love.

She felt his deep relief. *Thank God.*

She wanted to sit up, but she felt too shaky to manage it. She was lying in a pile of brown and orange leaves under the trees, and Jonah eased down beside her, his arms around her.

The change of scenery was confusing. "What happened?"

"I brought us back to my time. All three of us, I mean. I

guess while we were traveling, the two of you merged. "But I didn't know if it would be you or her who arrived back here."

"Me."

His eyes shimmered as he buried his face against her neck, breathing deeply.

"You smell good."

"It's the soap from your shower."

"No, it's you." He dragged in a breath and let it out. "It's been a hell of a few weeks, knowing we had to do this but not sure if we could pull it off."

"I'm sorry."

"Don't be."

"I made our lives hell."

"But look what we accomplished. Something nobody else has ever done." Just then, his cell phone rang, and he swiped the screen to answer. Frank Decorah was on the other end of the line.

"Put me on speaker," he said.

Jonah complied.

"I take it you succeeded," his boss said.

"How do you know?"

"All the newspaper articles and the references on the Web to the missing women are gone."

"But you remember?" Jonah asked.

"Everybody here remembers. But I think as far as the rest of the world is concerned, nobody knows you saved six women's lives—Alice's and five others."

"And we didn't change history?"

"Just a few minor things."

"Well, it's sinking in that we saved the other victims. And I'm so glad," Alice murmured. "But how did I hook up with Decorah if Jonah didn't rescue me from captivity?"

"We brought you in as a consultant."

"On what?"

"Computer research."

"But I don't know. ." Her voice trailed off. "I guess I do."

"And here's a bit of trivia you may like. One of those minor changes." He flashed a picture onto Jonah's screen. It was of a red brick Georgian mansion with a portico held up by Doric columns.

She gasped. "That's his house, isn't it?"

"Yeah."

"But it burned down. Is that an old picture?"

"No. Because he died before he could carry out his private hunting fantasy, he never incarcerated anyone there. It's owned by another family member. She rents it out for wedding parties and other special occasions."

"Oh Lord. From private prison to weddings."

"You can go see it later. For now, I've made reservations for the two of you at a resort in Western Maryland—Snow Cap Lodge. They have skiing in the winter, but autumn is nice in the mountains, too. You can spend the week relaxing after what you've been through. Then come back ready to join our IT team. Or you could go back to teaching English. Your choice."

"I like the idea of working with you—if I can really be a help."

"Yes. And you'll also be good for some field work—based on your recent success." He added, "Enjoy your well-earned vacation. But, Jonah, do e-mail me a report of today's activities."

"Of course."

"And one more thing." Frank's voice turned serious, "No more going back and saving murder victims in the past. It's too dangerous. Just this little episode shows how the timeline can be changed."

Jonah and Alice stared at each other. "Yes," they both answered.

Frank clicked off, leaving Alice and Jonah alone.

He rolled her to her back, and lowered his mouth to hers for a long, lingering kiss.

She clung to him, thinking that this was where their life together really began. For weeks they'd been afraid they would lose each other. Now that fear was over.

Yes, he answered her unspoken thought as he explored the interior of her mouth and slipped his hand under her shirt to cup her breast. At his touch, her nipple beaded.

"Oh Lord," she moaned. In the next second her eyes flew open. "We're outside."

"True. But the camp is gone, and we're in a nice private grove of trees."

"Private?"

"Let's hope so, because I don't think I have the strength to walk anywhere."

"Uh huh."

"Too bad you aren't wearing a skirt," he murmured against her mouth as he undid the snap at the top of her pants and thrust his hand inside.

"Do women still wear skirts in this century."

"A few do. On special occasions."

She moaned again as he slid his hand downward, into her sex. He watched her face as he stroked her.

You know I'm ready for you.

Uh huh. But I'm enjoying seeing the heat in your eyes.

Don't make me desperate. She lifted her hips to help him get rid of her pants and panties as she worked on his belt buckle and the button behind it.

Quickly she freed him from his dark pants and squeezed and stroked his length, bringing him to the same fever pitch she felt.

They were in too much of a hurry to undress further. In

seconds he was inside her. And seconds after that, they both climaxed, calling out as intense pleasure swept through them.

He gathered her to him and rolled to his side, and they lay locked together, still kissing and caressing.

When she drew in a breath, he raised his head. "What?"

"We forgot about a condom."

"I thought we were using them because we didn't know if you could stay with me. But now you are, right?"

She felt his sudden tension. "Yes."

"Thank God." He cleared his throat. "So the next thing we should settle is—when are we getting married?"

"When do you want?"

"As soon as possible."

"I guess this is as good a time as any to test out that ID Decorah got for me."

She hugged him to her, so glad that the uncertainty hanging over them was gone—and they were free to live the lives that . . ."

The lives that were our destiny, he said in her mind, repeating her thought. *Even though we met on a reality radio show.*

She giggled and said aloud. "So if this place is private enough to make love, we might as well take advantage of it again."

"You read my mind," he agreed, bringing his mouth down to hers for a long, lingering kiss.

EPILOGUE

There was no way for Jonah to transport a vehicle into the past, so he and Alice simply appeared in a wooded area near the entrance of the Davenport farm.

She looked around and blinked, taking a deep breath of the crisp fall air. "Thank you for doing this."

"I understand why you wanted your parents to know you're not dead."

Her voice hitched. "But they are still going to be sad. This is the last time I can ever see them."

He squeezed her hand as they stood in the shadows, looking out at the cornstalks that had turned brown and the cows contentedly munching grass in a nearby field.

They were married now, and a lot had changed over the past year. Because Jonah had improved the garage considerably, he'd been able to sell it at a nice price—along with most of his vehicles, since he now had better things to do in his spare time than fix cars. But he and Alice both wanted to keep the Chevy—of course.

With the cash, they'd bought a house not far from the Decorah offices. But Jonah had sensed a restlessness in his bride, and after much prompting, she had told him what was bothering her—the idea that her parents thought her life had been cut off all too early. He'd told her there might be a way to remedy that.

They'd talked to Frank, and he'd said they could visit her parents—once. But they would have to follow strict rules when they did it. She had understood and agreed.

Jonah was wearing jeans, a white tee shirt, a leather jacket and sneakers. She was wearing a pale green shirtwaist dress, a classic blazer, and loafers with white socks.

"Ready?" he asked.

"As ready as I'll ever be."

They stepped out into the sunshine and headed for the two-lane blacktop road she had traveled every time she left the farm. From there, they walked up the gravel lane that led to the simple Victorian two-story where Alice's family lived, and she waited around the side of the house while Jonah walked up to the front porch.

His heart was thumping as he trained his gaze on the door. It was 10:00 in the morning, and Alice had told him her father would have been up early and out to milk the cows and do some other chores. Then he liked to come in for some coffee with his wife. Her brothers and sister would be at school.

Hoping for no surprises, Jonah knocked on the door. After almost half a minute, a woman who looked a lot like an older version of Alice came to the door.

"Can I help you?" she asked as she wiped her hands on her apron.

"Mrs. Davenport, my name is Jonah Ranger. I have some news you'll want to hear—about your daughter, Alice," he said.

The woman put her hand to her mouth. "Alice was killed in a terrible accident a few months ago," she said.

"I'd like to talk to you about what really happened. Can I come in?"

Her lips trembled. "What are you saying?"

"I'd like to come in and talk to you and your husband, if I may," he repeated.

"Yes, yes, of course."

She stepped aside, and he followed her down the hall to a big country kitchen with a Formica and aluminum table, old gas range, refrigerator with a rounded top, and a stained porcelain sink—all of which Alice had described to him.

A man with the salt and pepper hair and the leathery features of someone who spent a lot of time outside was sitting at the table with a mug of coffee in front of him.

"Henry, this man says he has some information about our Alice."

Mr. Davenport stood slowly. He was tall and lean. Looking Jonah in the eye, he said, "What are you selling—a Bible with her name on the front? Her obituary encased in plastic?"

"I'm not selling anything. But I need to talk to you about Alice. It's important."

Mr. Davenport braced his large hands on his hips. "I'll give you one minute."

This was not going the way Jonah had anticipated, and he remembered the gun Alice had told him was in the top left drawer of the sideboard. He'd come to the house ahead of her so as not to give her parents a shock when they saw their daughter. Now he knew he couldn't ease into the subject.

"She's not dead," he blurted.

Mr. Davenport's eyes narrowed. "Is this some kind of trick?"

"No, let me talk to you for a few minutes."

The father still looked like he was going to pitch Jonah out the door, but his wife put a hand on his arm. "Henry, please. Let him speak his piece."

The father kept his gaze fixed on Jonah. "Go on, but this better be good."

"Alice wasn't killed in a rockfall. She was kidnapped by a man who wanted the world to think she was dead—so he could do what he wanted with her."

The mother gasped.

Jonah went on quickly. "But we discovered what had really happened and rescued Alice."

"Are you saying she's coming home?" Mr. Davenport demanded.

"Only for a short visit. The man who took her was involved in an international criminal conspiracy," he said, straying far from the truth now. "Alice would be in grave danger if he or his associates knew where she was. She's had to go into the witness protection program."

"What's that?" her father demanded.

"A federal government program that gives people new identities and a new life—to protect them. Alice is in it. She can't have any contact with her past. That would be very dangerous for her—and you, but she wanted you to know she was all right."

Should I come in now? Alice asked in his head.

Better do it before your father shoots me.

They all heard the front door open and looked toward the hall. Alice walked in. Her lower lip was trembling, and when she saw her parents, she was holding back tears.

"Alice?" her mother gasped.

Too overcome to speak, she nodded.

Her parents rounded the table, embracing her, and Jonah saw her clasp them tightly, holding on for long minutes before pulling away.

"I can't stay," she murmured. "But I wanted to see you—so much. Jonah and I worked out a way to visit—this once."

"You can't stay?" her father asked.

"I think he told you I couldn't." She moved to Jonah's side and reached for his hand. "I know this is all really hard to take in. This visit has to be a secret—to protect me—and you, too. But I wanted both of you to know I'm all right."

She gave them a watery smile. "Jonah and I are married. We're very happy together. We're living under assumed names —somewhere very far from here. But it's okay. The only hard part is that I have to stay hidden. That's an absolute must."

Mrs. Davenport had started to cry. Alice embraced her. "I know this is upsetting. Maybe it was a mistake to come."

Her father shook his head. "It's not a mistake. Seeing you is wonderful. If this visit is all we can have, we'll cherish it." He looked from her to Jonah and back again. "And he's really your husband?"

Alice nodded and held up her left hand, showing them a diamond engagement ring and a gold band.

Jonah saw her mother looking carefully at the two of them, judging the quality of their relationship. He pulled Alice closer and slung his arm around her waist.

"I'm lucky I found her," he said. "You raised a wonderful daughter."

"I just wanted to you to know I'm fine—and that I love you. And I wanted to see you one last time." As she spoke, she hugged both her parents.

"One last time," her mother repeated, her voice breaking.

"We can't stay," Jonah said. "This is bending the rules as it is."

"I understand," her father said to Jonah, finally coming to terms with the situation. "I appreciate your doing this."

"Mom, Dad, be happy for me. I found a man I never would have met if I hadn't gotten into trouble, and I wanted you to know everybody's fine."

Her parents were teary-eyed. "We love you," both of them said.

Jonah could see how torn up they were, and he hated to

leave them now. But after their previous adventures, he and Alice both knew that traveling back to make any changes could be dangerous to the timeline.

Jonah reached for her hand, and she clutched his fingers tightly.

We'd better go before I start weeping.

Yes.

Alice embraced her parents once more. Jonah watched her tear herself away before they turned and headed back to the door. Exiting the house, they walked down the lane together, heading for the twenty-first century and the life they had made together.

ALSO BY REBECCA YORK

SCIENCE FICTION ROMANCE

Off-World Series

Hero's Welcome (an off-world series short story)

Nightfall (an off-world series novella)

Conquest (an off-world series short story)

Assignment Danger (an off-world novella)

Christmas Home (an off-world short story)

Firelight Confession (an off-world novella)

Escape Velocity

PARANORMAL ROMANTIC SUSPENSE

Decorah Security Series

On Edge (a Decorah Security prequel novella)

Dark Moon (a novel)

Dark Powers (a novel)

Rx Missing (a novel)

Found Missing (a novel)

Hunter (a novel)

Trapped (a novel)

Scene of the Crime (a novel)

Hollow Moon (a novella)

Fire on the Moon (a novel)

Terror Mansion (a novella)

At Risk

Hunting Moon

Preying Game

ABOUT THE AUTHOR

 A New York Times and USA Today Best-Selling Author, Rebecca York is a 2011 recipient of the Romance Writers of America Centennial Award. Her career has focused on romantic suspense, often with paranormal elements.

Her 16 Berkley books and novellas include her nine-book werewolf "Moon" series. KILLING MOON was a launch book for the Berkley Sensation imprint. She has written over 50 books for Harlequin Intrigue, many in her popular 43 Light Street series.

She has written for Harlequin, Berkley, Dell, Tor, Carina Press, Silhouette, Kensington, Running Press, Tudor, Pageant Books, Scholastic, and Sourcebooks.

Her many awards include two Rita finalist books. She has two Career Achievement awards from Romantic Times: for Series Romantic Suspense and for Series Romantic Mystery. And her Peregrine Connection series won a Lifetime Achievement Award for Romantic Suspense Series.

Many of her novels have been nominated for or won RT Reviewers Choice awards. In addition, she has won a Prism Award, several New Jersey Romance Writers Golden Leaf awards and numerous other chapter awards.

Oliver Heber Books is now publishing her Decorah Security Series, her Off World Series, and her Soulmated Series.

* 9 7 8 1 6 4 8 3 9 8 5 5 1 *